CHRISTMAS AT YULETIDE FARM

MEGAN SQUIRES

For Brad.
Thank you for being my sturdy and proud evergreen through all of
the seasons of life.

DEACON

"Don't you dare lift your leg on that tree, Rascal!"

The Labrador dropped the leg in question and sauntered up to the next rotund Douglas fir, readying to test his luck a second time.

"I'm not fooling around, Rascal. You're gonna sleep on the porch if you insist on pushing it. I'm in no mood for your shenanigans today, dog. No mood."

Deacon Winters clucked his tongue and spurred the buckskin horse beneath him further down the hill. Hundreds of firs hemmed them in, a prickly barricade that sloped and meandered into the valley of their Northern California Christmas tree farm in rivers of deep green. While Deacon took a visual inventory, Rascal did figure eights between the horse's legs, doing his level best to trip up the mare. Luckily, at least one animal had a mind to obey its owner. Bella moseyed on without giving the dog even an ounce of the attention he so desperately sought, her hooves clacking a melodic beat that felt like a song.

Deacon noted the shiny green needles fanning out on the thick branches surrounding them, an indicator of healthy, well-cared-for trees. Forty-seven weeks of watering, pruning and tending to led to only one loss. While that was an overwhelming success in the grand scheme of things, it was still news he'd rather not break to the Browning family. Year after year, they'd been good fosters of their rental tree, always following the directions on the tag to keep it alive and thriving during the holiday seasons. Still, despite Deacon's best efforts, that particular fir tree bit the dust. Even though he had a beautiful replacement selected for the family, he felt the disappointment of that failure in his chest like a stubborn bout of heartburn.

"Let's head back up to the house," he said to his animals after making a mental note of the few trees that would need a little extra care the following day. "I bet supper's already on." Deacon collected the worn, oiled leather reins that had once belonged to his grandfather and swiveled around to angle Bella back up the mountainside. Without looking over his shoulder, he hollered, "Don't even think about it, Rascal!" and the little grunt of frustration from the retriever confirmed he'd been caught in another act of disobedience. That dog sure took every opportunity given to do precisely the wrong thing.

It was half-past-six when Deacon finally got Bella unsaddled, groomed, and settled into her stall for the night, a pile of hay and an oatmeal cookie as her reward for clocking in another hard day's work on the tree farm. Though everything in him wrestled against it, those rounded, pleading puppy eyes that blinked his direction turned Deacon into a bundle of mush. He chucked a cookie at Rascal and grimaced.

"Don't go getting any ideas that you actually earned that," he warned as he heaved the rolling barn door shut, the dog trotting haughtily on his heels. "I catch you trying to relieve yourself on another one of our trees and you'll be eating nothing but broccoli for a week. You hear me?"

Rascal waggled his floppy black ears.

"Hmph," Deacon grunted. His big body hugged close to the side of the barn as he trudged toward the main house at the very crest of the hill. It had started to snow, delicate little flecks sprinkling from the heavens that stuck to the wide brim of his cowboy hat and dusted the shoulders of his tan, canvas jacket. They dissolved only seconds after they appeared, like the popping of tiny bubbles on the surface of a still pond. This was the kind of snow Deacon tolerated. He preferred it over the dumping they'd received the week prior, the one that caused once-sturdy branches to bend and sag under a heavy, wet accumulation of slush. He knew their trees could easily withstand the temperamental winter weather—they were native to these parts, after all—but deliveries were slated to begin the following week. He needed their Christmas trees at their absolute best when they showed up on their customers' doorsteps. Nothing less would do.

The Yuletide Tree Farm was over seventy-five years

in the making and Deacon would not be the Winters to tarnish that hard-won heritage of excellent service, superior quality trees, and homegrown tradition. Plus, it had been his idea to add living tree rentals to their farm some five years ago. At the time, it was a suggestion met with more than one speculatively raised eyebrow. No one had even heard of such a thing. But when Tuff Winters, the farm's patriarch and Deacon's beloved grandfather, passed away one starless summer night after a valiant fight with cancer, legacy traded hands.

Deacon was now the owner of the farm. In the end, it was his decision—and his only—to make. Every year that went by, Deacon prayed he'd made the right one.

Shrugging out of his snow sodden coat as he stepped over the threshold and into the farmhouse, Deacon nudged the front door closed with a broad shoulder. Christmas music played quietly from his mother's antique radio that popped and crackled due to the poor mountain reception. Even with the overlay of white noise, the familiar carols brought about as much warmth as the cozy temperature of the home. He'd been chilled to the bone to the point of numbness, yet could feel himself gradually begin to thaw with each step further into the house.

"Smells delicious."

Deacon followed his nose toward the mouthwatering aroma of roasted carrots, savory pearl onions, and buttery Yukon potatoes like a hound on a scent trail. As he hoped it would, it led him to the dining room in the back of the house where his mother and brother gathered around the rustic, wide-plank table he'd built with his dad nearly a decade earlier using only timber found on their land.

"What is it? Pot roast?" Deacon lowered his hat to his chest before bending to place a kiss on his mama's cheek, then refit it where it belonged. He drew in another hearty breath and could almost taste the meal before him, the spices so delectable his stomach began to rumble.

"Close. Beef stew." Marla Winters took her eldest son's jacket and folded it over the crook of her arm, then gave him a firm poke in his side with her free hand. "I'm glad you finally decided to grace us with your presence. Cody's ready to dig in. Told him we'd give you ten more minutes before starting in without you." She placed the jacket over the back of an empty chair and cut Deacon a stern look before adding, "We expected you before sundown, Deacon."

"Got caught up checking the trees."

"Nothing that couldn't wait until morning," she insisted. She wiped her palms on an apron that had holly berries embroidered across the fabric. "You need to at least take your phone with you. What if I had to get ahold of you?"

"Then you could send Tilly out to fetch me."

Marla snorted. "That old dog is half deaf, all blind, and completely senile."

"And still, she's a more useful dog than Rascal."

As though he could comprehend the defamatory conversation, Rascal lifted his head from his curled up position next to Marla's dog in front of the pellet stove and let out an indignant groan.

"Not everything needs to be useful to be worthy. Rascal's a fine dog. Jenny sure loved him."

The hairs on Deacon's neck stood on end like he'd rubbed them with a static-covered balloon. Ignoring the unpleasant sensation and his mother's equally unpleasant statement, he scraped the dining chair out from underneath the table and plopped down with a huff.

"I've got the new farmhand coming tomorrow." Marla switched subjects, passing off a filled bowl of steaming, hearty stew and then gathering another to prepare one for herself. "Need you to see to it that the barn loft is tidied up and good to go. Clean sheets are in the dryer and extra TP is in the basement."

"Another one of the Carlton boys?"

Every holiday season, the tree farm would employ a few extra hands to help out during the inevitable rush. Deacon appreciated the additional support and hoped to have a returning worker join them again this year. Training someone entirely new often proved to be more trouble than it was worth.

"Not exactly." Marla's voice pitched an octave.

"What does 'not exactly' mean?" Deacon didn't like the knowing glint in his mother's eye. He studied her with scrutiny but her expression didn't give away much.

"Nothing." She shrugged as she took her seat across the table and collected her sons' hands, readying to say grace. "But it might not be a bad idea to spruce up the place a bit. You know, make it a little more inviting. Cozy."

"Why would it need to be inviting?"

Marla's mouth spread into a slow, steady grin before she shut her eyes to give thanks for their meal. "I think once you meet this particular farmhand, you'll understand."

KATE

"I don't like the angle of this footage." Kate Carmichael chewed on the cap of her ballpoint pen and spoke around it when she added, "You were right, Toby. We should have filmed in the morning and not the late afternoon. Those shadows are seriously so harsh. Looks like I have two raccoon eyes."

"I knew you weren't going to like it, which is why I had a separate camera set up off to the side the entire time." Toby Peyton moved the mouse across the pad and clicked out of the current window to maximize a different file. Another video clip from their latest assignment filled the entirety of the computer screen. "Do I know you, or do I know you?"

"After working together for seven years, I would say you know me better than anyone." Kate stood from the office chair and gave Toby's shoulders a quick, friendly squeeze. "Sometimes I think you might even know me better than I know myself. Now, where did I...?"

"Bookcase." Reading her mind, Toby flicked his index finger to point toward the shelving unit against the opposite wall. "Third shelf."

Kate's gaze zoomed about the room and locked in on her momentarily misplaced car keys, right where she'd left them at the start of her shift. "See? Seriously, what would I do without you?"

"I hate to say it, but you're about to find out. Courtney hasn't told you yet?"

"Hasn't told me what?" Brow drawn, Kate narrowed her gaze on her favorite cameraman the very moment Courtney Druthers, their Channel 14 News producer, waltzed into the room, stiletto heels clicking sharply across the tiled floor. The woman's ears must've been burning because her timing was nothing short of impeccable.

"Thought you were heading up the hill soon." Courtney came to a stop right next to Kate. She pressed her backside to the large work desk, crossing her legs at the ankles as she cocked her head to eye her employee. Courtney had two hairstyles in her arsenal —a sleek ponytail pulled so taut it made her eyebrows lift several inches higher on her forehead, or a flat-ironed bob that didn't shift even when her head did. Today, her blunt cut hung down to her outdated shoulder pads. "I expected you to be on the road by now."

"I was just about to head out when Toby dropped a rather disappointing bombshell. He's not going to be working with me on this assignment?"

"Correct." Courtney's glossy lips pressed into a flat,

decisive line. "I moved him over to the election fraud piece."

"Why? I thought Diego was on that."

"Diego's out of commission for the unforeseeable future. Snowboarding incident. Broke both legs and four ribs. Six teeth, too."

Kate winced. "Ouch."

"Yes. Ouch," Courtney deadpanned. The woman had always been no-nonsense in an off-putting and unapproachable way. That made for working relationships filled with noticeably more friction than harmony.

"Then who are you going to assign to my piece?" It wasn't that Kate didn't like working with the other cameramen at the station. Channel 14 had the best in the Sacramento valley, no question about it. She just loved the camaraderie she'd easily developed with Toby. In this industry, she found that was often hard to come by, even harder to keep around.

"That's the thing, Kate. I'm not assigning anyone."

"You're not assigning anyone." Kate chuckled an incredulous laugh that lifted the blonde wisps of hair framing her face. She curled her hand around her ear to tuck away the errant strands. "Right."

"I'm serious." Courtney's features hardened along with her tone. "We've started the hiring process, but it'll be at least two weeks until I have someone I can throw at your assignment."

Kate did the quick math. "Two weeks puts us out too far. This is a holiday special. It won't give us enough time to get everything buttoned up and ready to air before Christmas."

"Exactly. Which is why I'm putting the ball completely in your court."

"What does that mean?" Kate was unquestionably confident in her reporting skills; she always had been. She'd graduated summa cum laude from college, double majoring in journalism and communications, and the many awards she earned as the area's top reporter only bolstered her self-assurance. She was excellent at reporting the news, but that did little good if she didn't have someone there to film her while she reported it.

"I'm relying on you to see this project through from start to finish." Courtney clicked her holiday-colored nails on the ledge of the table, a tap-tap-tapping sound that made Kate's jaw tick. "*On the Job with Kate Carmichael* is about to become a one-woman show. You've been a sushi chef, an embalmer, a sommelier. Surely you can do this, too."

Kate's head spun faster than a pirouetting Sugar Plum Fairy. "You do realize I didn't really *become* those things. Just reported on what it's like to be them. Plus, I still don't even understand what you're saying. Without a cameraman, how am I going to capture life as a Christmas tree farmer? Do you just expect me to film everything with…what? My phone?"

"That's *exactly* what I expect you to do." Courtney pushed off the table and sauntered back toward the door before pausing in the frame. "Cora in IT will help you manage the social media aspect of things. All we need is for you to provide her with the daily content."

"*Daily* content?"

"That's correct. We're thinking of trying something

new with your segment. We'll be taking it completely online. Rather than creating a packaged piece to deliver at the end of your assignment, we want to follow you day-to-day. It's no secret people are going online for their news more often than not lately. We think your piece is a perfect fit to test this out."

"I'm not some social media influencer, Courtney. I'm a seasoned, award-winning reporter."

"Then this should be a piece of cake for you." Flipping her wrist over, Courtney tapped on the face of her watch. "And you really should be on the road by now. They are expecting you by three."

KATE HAD CLENCHED HER TEETH THROUGHOUT THE entire drive and felt the repercussions of that as a throbbing ache in her molars. Even when she rubbed her jaw, the pain didn't subside. Killing the engine of her sedan, she reclined in the driver's seat a moment, meditating on her situation and breathing deep like she'd learned to in her yoga classes.

A wooden sign bearing the name *Yuletide Tree Farm* hung over the entrance immediately to her left. It swayed on its hinges from a gusty wind that rocked it back and forth like an abandoned swing. It would've been eerie if not for the festive, holiday lettering and the clumps of snow that capped the corners in just the right places.

Kate rolled her window down a crack and inhaled the fresh mountain air that seeped into the cab of her vehicle. She had always loved the Sierras. As a little girl, she would often vacation in the Lake Tahoe area with her family, spending her summers on the crystal blue waters and her winters on the powdery slopes. But travel outside of work was a luxury she hadn't been afforded in recent years. Maybe that was the reason she had subconsciously picked this particular tree farm, located just minutes from Tahoe near the neighboring town of Truckee. She knew her jam-packed calendar wouldn't allow for a winter getaway, so she would have to fit one into her work schedule instead. It was a win-win. Or it had been, until Courtney pulled the rug out from under her.

Groaning, Kate fished her phone from her handbag and flipped the screen around. She winced when her face came into view. This was not what she had signed up for, but there was a clear challenge in Courtney's tone that Kate couldn't shake. While her boss's words indicated her confidence in Kate's abilities, her inflection conveyed anything but that. The opposite, in fact. For that very reason, Kate was determined to knock this assignment right out of the park. She wouldn't let an unanticipated change in direction derail everything she'd worked for, even if Kate had recently questioned whether or not the station would be her permanent landing place, profession-wise. Admittedly, she'd grown a bit restless in recent years.

Pressing the record button, she straightened in her seat and started right in.

"Good afternoon, Sacramento!" she began as she smiled broadly into the phone's small camera. "Kate

Carmichael here and once again, I'm on the job to bring you an inside look at some of the most interesting, note-worthy and uncommon professions around. As you'll see, this month we've added a bit of holiday flair. While many of us are still trying to work off that recent Thanksgiving meal, for others, the Christmas season is already in full swing. And there's no other place where that is more evident than here at Yuletide Tree Farm, located in the snowy hills of Northern California. Over the next two weeks, I'll be bringing content a little differently than we have in the past. Each day, you'll be able to follow my journey online as I learn just what it takes to be a Christmas tree farmer. I'll be chronicling my experience with my camera and will post daily for you to view, share, and leave a comment on. I'm excited about this new and interactive opportunity to share my experiences as they play out, while also giving you a firsthand look at the tree farming industry. So put on your Santa caps, Sacramento, because it's sure beginning to look a lot like Christmas!"

Kate hit the button again and tossed the phone to her lap.

"Well, that was ridiculous," she muttered under an exasperated breath.

This was going to be a much larger challenge than she had ever anticipated.

DEACON

"Just slapped another coat of paint on the reindeer cutouts but I think we'll have to completely replace them next year. They're looking a little shoddy. Had to reattach three different antlers and one red nose." Cody Winters flicked the bristles of the wet paintbrush against his thigh, then jammed it into his back pocket. "What next?"

Deacon's eyes focused on his younger brother and then down at the clipboard in his hands. There were roughly a thousand jobs to complete and just under two days to do them. Even Santa and his magical elves couldn't crank out this list in time.

He grunted. "Are the parking cones out yet?"

"Yep. Did that this morning."

"And the outhouses?"

"Ordered those, too. They'll be dropped off tomorrow afternoon."

Opening up the tree farm to the public was no small

feat. It took hours of planning and preparation, along with flexibility and ingenuity when something would inevitably go wrong. He wanted to say they'd become a well-oiled machine over the years, but that was a stretch. More like a clunky, sputtering engine that did its best to make things work.

"What about the tree funnels?"

Cody slapped a palm squarely between Deacon's shoulder blades that shoved him forward a bit with the movement. "Already hauled all five of those out of the storage barn. And the netting will be here Friday. We'll be rocking and rolling and ready to open things up come Saturday morning."

Deacon wasn't so sure about that, but he liked his brother's confidence.

"Sorry you had to do all of that on your own," Deacon apologized. "I really thought our farmhand would be here by now."

"I am! I'm right here!"

At the sound of the high pitched voice, the two men whirled around. There, just under their farm entrance sign, was a woman scurrying across the gravel in wobbly heels that were good for nothing but twisting ankles.

"I'm so sorry. I set out on the road later than I'd planned. Got caught in traffic coming over the hill." She came to a stop right in front of the bewildered Winters men and shoved a hand into the empty space. "Kate Carmichael."

Deacon exchanged a look with his brother. "*You're* the farm hand?"

"Yup." She took hold of his gloved hand when he

hesitantly offered it and gave an overly enthusiastic shake. "Here to be of service and to learn all things tree farm related."

"Just to get things straight, you were hired on by Marla Winters to help us around the farm for the holiday season?"

The woman thumbed her chin as though really pondering the question, then dropped her hands and shrugged. "Yes. I think that was her name but I'm not one-hundred percent sure. I'd have to look back at my notes."

"Yuletide Tree Farm?"

"Right." She nodded in slow motion, like maybe Deacon was the one having a difficult time under-standing things. "Yuletide Tree Farm. The very one."

Slapping his shoulder again before jogging backward and giving his older brother a salute, Cody said, "I'll leave you to sort this one out, brother."

Just like Cody to leave Deacon high and dry when it came to dealing with employees. Cody was great managing tasks and to-do's, less great with managing people. Not that Deacon was any better. Their father had been the people-person in the family, a trait he'd failed to pass down to his sons.

Kate dug out her phone from within her purse and looked up at Deacon with a wide, innocent gaze that bore a glimmer of hope Deacon couldn't pinpoint. "Before we get started, I was hoping to interview you. Nothing fancy. Just a quick little Q&A."

Deacon all but choked, a laugh getting wedged dead-center in his throat. "*You* want to interview *me*? I'm pretty sure my mother took care of the interviewing process when she lined things up for you to work here."

A small line creased the space between Kate's eyebrows. "I'm sorry, but I think there's been some sort of misunderstanding."

That was evident. "Yes. I agree."

"Your mother didn't tell you who I am?"

This was getting ridiculous. "Listen. Kate, is it?"

She nodded excitedly. "Yes. Kate. Kate Carmichael."

"Okay, Kate Carmichael. As far as I'm concerned, the interviewing process already occurred. If my mother thought you'd be fit to work the farm with us this season, then so be it. I don't quite see it, what with the stilettos and designer handbag, but that's none of my concern. So long as you've got a pair of boots in your luggage and some grit stowed away in that small frame of yours, you'll get on just fine."

"So she *didn't* tell you who I am."

"No, but you already have. Kate Carmichael. We've been over this a couple times now."

The woman looked up at Deacon, laughter alight in blue eyes so intense he had to blink just so he didn't stare. They were the exact color of the deepest part of his beloved Lake Tahoe. "And that doesn't sound the slightest bit familiar to you at all?"

Deacon pulled his hat from his head and raked a hand through matted hair that was in need of a good trim. "Is it supposed to?"

"*On the Job with Kate Carmichael?*"

He shook his head, his expression as blank as fresh snowfall.

"Nothing?"

"Listen, Kate. I've got a whole heap of things to do and playing this *'guess my identity'* game isn't on the list. Head on up to the barn loft and get yourself situated and when you're ready to work—and dressed appropriately for it—come back down."

"Okay." She vacillated. "Sure. But I'd still really like to interview you first if you'll just give me five minutes."

Deacon's hands shot into the air. "I don't understand why you insist on interviewing me! I'm the boss here. I do the interviewing. Now please, go get ready."

"This news segment is going to be really boring if it's just me talking into the camera."

"What on earth are you talking about?"

"The piece I'm doing about your tree farm for Channel 14 News. It's going to be a real snooze if I can't get some decent footage and insider info from the guy actually running the place."

Like a crossing guard, Deacon lifted a halting hand. "Hold on." He pinched his eyes shut for the measure of a breath before reopening them but his jaw remained clenched, even when he spoke. "I need to go conduct an interview of my own real quick."

"Yeah?" Kate's tone lifted. "Who with?"

His mouth turned downward when he answered in an irritated, cross voice, "My mother."

❄

"What would make you think any part of this was a good idea?"

Marla didn't lift her eyes from the wreath in front of her. She'd made over a dozen already and placed them in various nooks and crannies within the small, on-site store they operated during the holidays. There were glittering ornaments bearing their farm name hung on a recently harvested tree standing proud in the corner. Denim, button-up shirts and trucker hats with their logo filled a chipped, red bookcase on the far wall. Instrumental holiday music played softly over the speakers and Marla hummed along with the well-known tunes, her voice sweet, melodic, and as comforting as an heirloom quilt. Next week, they'd get a delivery of candles from their favorite maker and that would catapult the shop to an entirely new level of holiday cheer. The sights, the sounds, and the smells of Christmas would fill their farm store completely to the brim.

Deacon loved this little space, but right now he couldn't afford any distraction from his mission. He needed answers. *Pronto*.

"Mom," Deacon repeated, his patience worn paper thin. "Seriously, what is going on here?"

Tucking a fresh evergreen sprig into the chicken wire frame, Marla held up the wreath and smiled approvingly at her workmanship. "This is my best one yet. Still not as good as Grandma Kay's, but I think she'd be proud. Don't you?"

"Huh?" Deacon yanked his hat from his head and speared his fingers through his hair. "Yes. Sure. It looks great." He shoved the hat back on and took a step closer.

"Mom, I really need answers. Who is this Kate Carmichael and why is she here?"

"Oh! So you've met Kate?" Marla's lips spread into a grin that was two parts devilry, one part innocence.

"Yes, I met Kate."

"And what did you think?" Walking away while she spoke, Marla gathered the finished wreath and placed it onto an empty wall hook, right next to a painted wooden sign that read *Farm Fresh Christmas Trees*.

"Based on the way she was dressed and how unprepared she seemed for a day on the farm, I'd say she's about the least qualified hand you've hired yet. And that's saying a lot, Mom. Mack Hudson was a train wreck."

"I liked Mack." Marla smiled wistfully as she adjusted the big red bow on the wreath. "He had some focus issues, I'll give you that. But he was a good kid. Nice family."

"Sure. Fine. He was fine. But really, Mom, why this Kate woman?"

Moving to the register and instructing her son to follow with a small beckoning wave, Marla opened the drawer. She removed a handful of papers from beneath the till, gave them a troubled glance, and then slid them across the counter toward Deacon.

"What's this?" He gathered the sheets and flipped through them hastily.

"Our numbers from the last five years."

"I know our numbers, Mom." He dropped the pile and pushed them back. "I do our books."

"Then you'd know that our income was down the

last two years running." She removed her wire reading glasses from her nose and tucked them into her shirt pocket before crossing her arms over her chest as though bracing herself to deliver the news. "And you'd also know that eighty-percent of our sales are from customers residing within a twenty-mile radius of the farm."

"Yes. I know that."

"So don't you think it's time to broaden our reach?"

It probably was, but they'd been getting on just fine. And if Deacon were being honest, he didn't have the skills required—nor the interest necessary—to dump any time or money into a big-scale marketing plan. He knew how to grow, harvest, sell, and deliver trees. He didn't know the first thing about promotion.

"It probably wouldn't be a bad idea to expand our reach a little," he ultimately conceded.

"I'm glad you agree. That's why I picked Kate. It's a win-win all around."

Deacon shook his head. "I'm still not understanding—"

"*On the Job with Kate Carmichael* has a viewership of over twenty-thousand people. You know I'm no good at math, but I did a little calculating and if just five-percent of those viewers headed up the hill to buy their trees from us, that would amount to a thousand new customers. We've certainly got the inventory. We just need the publicity," Marla explained, like this was something she'd spent a long time pondering. "And Kate's comes for free."

Deacon blew out a long, slow sigh. "Not entirely

free. It'll cost us—in the form of more work placed on my shoulders during an already hectic time."

"Why are you so quick to write this woman off? For all we know, she could be an incredibly hard worker. In fact, I'd put money on it. This is what she does, you know. Job training to learn new skills so she can report back on her television show. She's a bit of a renaissance woman, if you ask me."

"That's just it, Mom. I didn't ask you. Not to hire this woman and certainly not to have our farm filmed and under a microscope when what we really need to do is focus on our trees and our customers."

"Give her a chance, Deacon," Marla pleaded, covering her son's hands with her own. He ignored the wink his mother tacked on when she added, "Kate Carmichael just might surprise you."

KATE

Kate chucked her favorite pair of heels across the room, wincing when they collided with a wooden picture frame holding a photo of what had to be the Winters family. There were at least a dozen people within the shot, all wearing denim pants, crisp white shirts, and matching smiles. Her eyes hung on Deacon who stood a good half-foot taller than the rest, his imposing stature making him the most prominent. He had an arm slipped over the shoulder of a beautiful brunette and a happy looking dog at his feet. Deacon appeared content. Joyful. The polar opposite of the man she'd been introduced to just moments earlier.

"Sorry," Kate apologized to no one in particular as she righted the frame and collected her discarded shoe.

Flopping back onto the bed, and sinking into the lumpy mattress, she stared up at the barn loft ceiling. Cobwebs wove into the corners like forgotten Halloween decorations that never made their way back into storage boxes. There was an unlit candle perched on the night-stand and the thick layer of dust coating the wax hinted it was more for looks than function. At least the quilt was soft and the pillows firm. This loft certainly couldn't be mistaken for a popular weekend rental. In fact, Kate would be surprised to learn if anyone had stayed in it since the previous holiday season. Still, she would just have to make do.

Deacon seemed glaringly unimpressed by her pres-ence. She wasn't about to put up a fuss about her living quarters and give him any sort of justification for that outlandish reaction. She made a mental note to look for a broom and a duster the next morning to take care of things on her own. In no time flat, the barn would be cleaned up and feeling just like home, not that her own downtown address held any more significance.

Just as she was about to unpack her limited belong-ings, she heard the buzz of an incoming call from her phone nestled on the nightstand. When she saw the name on the screen, a grin burst onto her face.

"Toby!" she shouted into the receiver upon answering.

"Just wanted to make sure you made it to the tree farm okay."

Kate wedged the phone between her jaw and shoulder as she made quick work of unpacking her things and stowing them into an old oak dresser, one of the few pieces of furniture in the little room. "You're so sweet to check on me. I did. Safe and sound."

"And how is the place?"

Pulling back the sheer curtain on the only window in

the loft, Kate cast her gaze out over the rolling hills swathed in deep forest green. "The farm is absolutely beautiful. Feels like Christmas everywhere you look. Evergreen trees for days."

"Shouldn't be too much of a challenge to get some great footage of that, then. If you need any pointers or tips, I'm just a phone call away. I'm happy to help however I can. I still feel bad that I can't be there with you."

"I appreciate that, Toby. And you're right; I won't have any trouble with that side of things. It's the interviewing portion that I think is going to be the real struggle."

"You think so? But that's your bread and butter."

"You wouldn't believe the guy that runs the place. Apparently, he had no idea I was even coming here to begin with. His mother hired me without his knowledge —or approval—it seems. He's not keen on me being here, much less recording any part of my experience. I've really got my work cut out for me with this."

Kate could hear the reassuring smile in Toby's voice when he said, "If there's anyone that can do it, Kate, it's you."

"I appreciate the vote of confidence, Toby," she said. "I should probably head on down before I get scolded for taking too long to get ready."

"I don't want to keep you. Just know I'm here if you need me. You've got this."

Kate beamed as they exchanged their goodbyes. She had relied on Toby over the years not just as her cameraman, but as a sounding board and confidant. In truth, the man had practically become her security blanket. While she knew things would be easier with him at her side, maybe this was exactly the push she needed to finally propel herself out of her well-worn comfort zone.

Either way, she had no real say in the matter.

Tugging a stiff boot onto each foot, Kate coiled her favorite green and red handmade scarf around her neck and descended the loft staircase, careful not to lose her footing on the creaky boards that threatened to fall right out from under her. She could hear soft snorting and nickering from further down the barn aisle, the silhouettes of two saddled horses coming into view the closer she stepped.

"You take this one," Deacon mumbled her direction once she was within earshot.

"Hello to you, too."

Rolling his eyes, Deacon turned his back as he tugged on a strap under the horse's belly to secure the saddle firmly into place. "I thought we already got all of the pleasantries out of the way."

"I wouldn't call anything about our first meeting pleasant."

Deacon dropped a heavy hand onto the saddle horn. He cut her a look that made her stomach feel like a piece of wet fabric being wrung out. "You ready to get to work?"

She'd expected some sort of snide comeback and was honestly a little surprised when he didn't readily give one. "Yep. I'm ready." Pointing a toe, she waved her hand toward her feet to show off her new kicks. "Boots and all."

"Sure, but that's about it."

"What's that supposed to mean?"

In one effortless maneuver, Deacon stepped up into one stirrup and swung a leg up and over to mount the horse. He looked just like a cowboy from the old, grayscale westerns Kate's grandfather watched when she would visit the convalescent home where he resided back when she was a child. There was something nostalgic in Deacon's movement that had Kate's heart squeezing at the memory. But when he opened his mouth to speak again, all of that reassuring familiarity flitted away. "That expensive jacket is going to be covered in pine needles."

Kate shrugged inside her wool peacoat. "This thing? It'll be fine."

"Suit yourself."

Hooking her hands on her hips, she added, "Well, it'll have to do because it's the only one I brought."

Deacon jabbed his heels into the sides of his horse and upon impact, the animal began walking steadily forward.

It had been years since Kate sat on the back of a horse and then it was only a short trail ride where her horse had, for all intents and purposes, been on autopilot. She didn't know the first thing about steering, guiding, or managing a thousand-pound animal.

And evidently, she didn't know how to get on top of one, either.

Grabbing the saddle with both hands, she attempted to pull herself onto the horse but her foot wedged awkwardly in the stirrup, hooking on the toe of her boot, and before she could process what was happening, she tipped up and over and landed flat on her backside in the slushy dirt below.

Deacon swiveled his steed around. "Really?"

"A little less judgment and a little more help would be nice." Kate tried to tug her foot from the stirrup that trapped it. Even her horse angled a sidelong glance as she struggled to free herself from the tangle.

With a huff of displeasure, Deacon slunk off his horse and clomped toward her, his feet heavy and frustrated breaths even heavier. "You're lucky Sarge is an old, spookless horse. You try that on any other animal and you would've been dragged a half-mile down the road." He shot a hand out toward her like the toss of a lifesaver into troubled waters.

"You think I ended up on the ground on *purpose*?" With his assistance, Kate got to her feet. She brushed off the back of her pants with two palms and yanked on the hem of her coat to try to appear somewhat presentable.

"I don't know. Isn't that what you reporters do? Add dramatic effect or something?"

Unbelieving, Kate stood there, shaking her head like a nervous tick. "You are unreal."

"I'm not the one in the fake news industry."

"Oh, please! I'm a journalist who reports on unusual jobs. I'm not some frontline investigator." She swiped her hands together before she tried—for a second time —to get into the saddle. "Would it be too much trouble to ask for some assistance?"

Before she could collect herself, Deacon had two huge hands on the curve of her waist and with the effort it would take to lift a feather, he all but tossed her onto the horse's back. She wasn't sure if it was from her previous efforts or from his unexpected touch, but a heated blush crawled up her neck and onto her face, warming her up by several degrees. "Oh. Thank you."

"Welcome," he muttered as he strode back to his waiting horse. "I got you into the saddle, but it's your job to stay there."

"I'll try my best."

Luckily, Sarge proved his worth and trailed uneventfully behind Deacon and his horse as they journeyed toward the thick forest of greenery.

"Where are we headed?" Kate called out. The horse hooves pulsed in a beat, a rhythm that was consistent despite everything around her being anything but. Kate typically did fine out of her element, but something about Deacon made her confidence blunder.

"Checking on our rental trees. We start deliveries next week."

"I remember reading on your website that you offer live trees for rent. Not too many farms do that, right?"

"Right," Deacon mumbled. He sure had a knack for buttoning up any conversation Kate tried to start.

"Do a lot of people sign up to rent them?"

"Uh huh."

Kate would've closed her eyes to collect her thoughts and composure if she hadn't been on top of a massive animal. Instead, she pursed her lips and silently counted to ten in an effort to regroup. It didn't do her any good to let frustration get the better of her here, she knew that full well. "How many people are currently enrolled in your rental tree program this year?"

"Fifty-three."

At least she got answers when she kept at it long enough. "And you deliver all the trees?"

"Yep."

She leaned back in her saddle for balance as the horses navigated the slope of the land, one hoof placed dexterously in front of the other on the steep terrain. "Do people get the same trees year after year?"

"Most of 'em."

"So they rent a specific tree for the holiday season and then you take care of it the rest of the year?"

"We do."

This was like pulling teeth, and not even wiggly teeth but those stubborn, immovable back molars.

"Shoot," Deacon blurted out of nowhere. "Donna's looking a little too thick around the middle. Dang it. Mindy, too."

Kate blanched. "Excuse me?"

"I said Donna's gotten real fat. Her proportions are all off."

"Well, goodness! Don't you think that's rather rude?"

For the first time since meeting, Kate heard a jovial sound escape Deacon's mouth. She couldn't be sure, but it sounded an awful lot like a laugh. "Calm down. I'm talking about the trees." He pointed toward the closest fir on their left-hand side. "That one belongs to Donna Palmerson. See how it's lost its shape? How it's too round in the middle and thin at the top? It'll swallow ornaments whole. We need to come through here tomorrow and do some final pruning before these are ready to leave the property."

"You call your trees by name?"

"I do. It makes them easier to identify. They've got nametags, but I've also got a spreadsheet that lists them all. I like it better than calling them by a number."

Scanning the tree closest to her for a tag, Kate perked up when she located it and said, "Jenny here is looking kind of scraggily."

Whatever semblance of rapport she felt developing between them was obliterated with that lone sentence.

"You don't get to comment on Jenny's tree." Deacon's voice felt like a reprimand.

"I'm sorry," she recanted, disliking the irrepressible waver in her tone. She held securely to the reins in her hands and gulped. "I just thought that we could pretty it up a little before delivering—"

"That tree isn't going anywhere." Deacon clucked his tongue and whipped his horse around, pointing it in the direction of the barn that sat like a beacon on the hilltop. "We're done here for today."

"But we just got started—"

"Breakfast is in the main house at 6:30. We'll begin working at 7:30 AM, sharp," he spoke over his shoulder as he spurred his horse into a trot like he was running away from both Kate and the conversation. Sarge picked up on the cue and jogged compliantly behind. With his face kept forward, Deacon added, "And don't think about showing up late like you did this afternoon."

DEACON

Deacon couldn't sleep. He'd tossed and turned so many times he felt like a pancake on a griddle. Not that he was a stranger to restlessness. In fact, he couldn't recall the last decent night of sleep he'd had since the skiing accident. The doctor had originally attributed it to his broken collarbone—that the physical discomfort was the reason for his inability to shut his eyes for more than five-minute intervals.

But Deacon knew it didn't take four years for bones to heal. That was the relatively quick and easy part. The healing of his heart had occurred at a much, much slower rate.

Surrendering to the insomnia, he shoved back his quilt and dropped his feet into the fuzzy slippers waiting at the side of his bed. He snagged a robe from the bedpost and wrapped it around his body before making his way down the long hall to the kitchen, eyes bleary and spirit heavier than Santa's gift sack of presents. His one and only mug had recently been washed and settled into the drying rack next to a single place setting that got more use than the matching seven collecting dust in his cupboard.

Deacon was a bachelor. He didn't need more than one of anything, really. A quaint, one-bedroom cottage he'd built with his own hands. One good horse. One dog. (The good part was debatable on that). One fulfilling job.

One woman to love.

He'd once had that woman and Deacon knew his chances of ever meeting someone to fill that void again was slim-to-none. He'd already used up his one shot.

Twisting the heels of his hands into his eyes, he blew out a sigh that woke Rascal from his dog bed.

"Sorry," Deacon apologized as he grabbed his mug and filled it with apple cider purchased from a local farm just a mile down the road. He punched a few numbers on the microwave and waited for his drink to heat. "You can go back to bed, Rascal."

The dog was fast asleep before Deacon had even finished the sentence. How he envied that—the ability to shut out the world with just one blink.

When the microwave dinged, he retrieved his steaming drink and hunkered onto the plush, leather couch in the living room. Snow fell on the other side of the picture windows, fluttering down in iridescent flakes that looked like the sugar crystals sprinkled atop a gingersnap cookie. The forecast called for sunshine by morning. Deacon was grateful for that. If it was going to storm, he preferred mother nature get it out of the way during the night. Come daylight, there would be chores to tackle and business to take care of. Everything was made easier under clear skies.

In just a few short hours, he'd have not only a seemingly insurmountable list of jobs to complete, but a new farmhand to deal with. What had his mother been thinking? He knew her heart was in the right place. It always was. But this Kate woman sure rubbed Deacon the wrong way. She'd marched onto the property, her head filled with notions as to how his farm fit into her story, not how she fit into his farm. It was hard to tell exactly who worked for whom.

He'd have to set her straight after a hearty breakfast and a couple hours of sleep under his belt. He knew the first full day on the job set the pace for the remainder of the harvest season. He wasn't about to let her believe her little news piece took precedence over selling trees. That just wouldn't work.

One mug of cider down and a half hour of wakefulness later, Deacon found himself with his laptop open and Kate Carmichael's name typed into the search bar. He had to laugh at how presumptuous she'd been during their introduction, like she was someone famous who deserved recognition. Even if she had been an Oscar winning actress, Deacon likely wouldn't have noticed. He didn't pay attention to things like that, didn't have time to waste in front of a movie screen or television set. He was a simple, hardworking man who used all of the available hours of the day for productivity.

Maybe that was the reason he gave himself a little

leeway when it came to researching Kate right then. It was night and he wasn't wasting anything other than the sleep that always eluded him anyway.

Before he knew it, he'd fallen into an *On the Job with Kate Carmichael* rabbit hole. Episode after episode of the woman learning new trades. Tennis coach. Rattlesnake removal specialist. Fortune cookie writer. He had to admit, it was undeniably entertaining. She had a charisma in front of the camera that he hadn't detected during their brief time together. She was confident and self-assured, not ruffled and harried like she had been when she'd tried to mount the horse and ended up with her feet in the air and her pride bruised.

She was a natural on camera.

But that didn't mean Deacon welcomed that camera on his property.

It was nearly sunrise when he finally snapped his laptop shut and allowed his eyes several moments of rest with his head leaned back on the couch cushion. If it hadn't been for Rascal's startling bark, alerting Deacon that he was late with the dog's morning bowl of kibble, he would've stayed asleep on that couch until noon. It was the first real sleep he'd had in weeks.

Blinking, Deacon's gaze came into focus on the hands on the clock hanging on the opposite wall.

"Oh no!" He jumped up from the couch. "Shoot!"

Rascal barked.

"Shoot. Shoot. Shoot!"

Bark. Bark. Bark!

In an all-out sprint, Deacon rushed across the room and scooped the dog's meal from the open bag. Bits of dry food rolled across the hardwood floor like scattered marbles, a mess he'd have to leave for later.

"Why didn't you wake me sooner?" Deacon gave Rascal a displeased look before heading to his room to throw on a pair of jeans, plaid work shirt, jacket and boots. He scrubbed a toothbrush over his teeth, then shoved his cowboy hat onto his head. It was the fastest he'd ever gotten ready, but it wouldn't do any real good. It was already 7:45.

Fresh snow crunched under his boots as he tramped down the hill toward the rambling main house. He could see thick coils of smoke twisting up from the red brick chimney but it was the rich, savory smell of bacon that reached him first. That was quickly followed by the joyful sound of laughter, something long absent from their mountaintop farm.

Deacon cracked the front door open and followed the pleasant sound into the dining room.

"Sometimes I do wish we had the chance to slow down a little during the holidays and just enjoy the season, but I wouldn't even know what that would look like. I've been doing this since I was a little girl—"

Marla twisted around in her chair when Deacon entered.

"Deacon. You're in the shot!" His mother threw her hands in the air and slapped them back down onto the table in a display of utter annoyance.

Not the greeting he'd expected. She brushed his hand away when he reached around her to snatch a piece of bacon from the greasy pile on her plate.

"Now I have to say all of that again!" Marla scowled at her son. "I'm sorry, Kate. Where were we?"

Deacon ignored his mother's words. "We need to get to work."

"I already am." Kate tapped the edge of her cell phone and propped it up in front of her, about to continue with Marla's interview. "Marla, you can just pick back up where you say you've been tree farming all of your life."

"I mean, it's time to do the job you were hired to do," Deacon corrected. He stole another piece of fatty bacon.

"That's the funny thing." Kate aimed her eyes at Deacon. "I've been hired for two things: work at a tree farm for the holiday season and document what that's like. I've technically got two jobs to do."

"Which is exactly what I'm concerned about. I can't have you putting in half the effort when I've got more than full-time work to be done around here."

"That's not going to be an issue," Kate volleyed. "When I do something, I give it one-hundred percent. I'll be giving both jobs that and more."

"You do realize there's no logic to that math, right?"

Kate rolled her lake-blue eyes. "You get what I mean." She pushed to her feet and collected her breakfast plate, along with Marla's now that Deacon had eaten all of her bacon and nothing remained on the empty ceramic. "If my short-term memory serves me correctly, I'm the one who was here and ready to go at 6:30. Over an hour and a half before you decided to waltz in."

"I overslept."

With an empathetic look that only a mother could perfect, Marla glanced up at her son. She took his large hand into hers and rested it on her shoulder. "You still having trouble sleeping? The doctor said he could prescribe you something for that."

Deacon cut his mother a fast look. "I'm fine."

Like she was suddenly privy to something she shouldn't be, Kate fumbled with the plates in her hands and then scooted into the kitchen, quick to duck out of the mother-son exchange.

"You can leave those at the sink, Kate. I'll take care of them," Marla instructed. She still had her hand on her son's and gave it a pat. "Deacon, there are people you can talk to. Professionals. Working through everything might help you sleep at night. I think it's about time to put it all in the past once and for all. Don't you?"

"I've worked through everything I need to work through." He pulled his hand free. "Now I need to get to real work."

"You know I only push it because I love you."

He fell silent a beat before he shed a small smile and said, "I know. I love you, too."

"Think about it. Please. You can't keep things bottled up inside you forever, son."

His mother might be right, but it sure wouldn't keep him from trying.

KATE

"I'm guessing an arborist isn't on the list of jobs you've tackled for your show."

Kate stepped back from the tree, pruners in hand. She was covered in so many needles it was hard to see the navy fabric of her jacket underneath. She nearly looked like some new breed of obscure porcupine. "Is it that bad?"

"People kinda like to be able to hang ornaments on their Christmas trees, you know. It's a bit of a tradition."

"I did cut the branches a little short, didn't I?"

Deacon chuckled, a sound so unexpected it almost made Kate jump. "If that was a haircut, you just gave it a buzz."

"Did I completely ruin it?"

"Honest answer?" There was a flicker in Deacon's eye that Kate couldn't pinpoint, a little speck of playfulness that had her stomach knotting. What was that all about? He'd been so frustrated earlier.

"Yes," she prodded. "Honest answer."

"Yeah. You totally ruined it." He took the pruners from her hand and shoved them into his back pocket like she couldn't be trusted with them anymore. "But that's why I had you practice on a tree we weren't planning to sell."

"In that case, I hope you have a few more I can practice on. I have a feeling it's going to take me several trial runs before I get this down." Kate's shoulders slumped. She didn't like failing at things and she'd failed spectacularly here.

The closest thing to a smile crossed Deacon's lips, quick and fleeting before his mouth fell into a neutral position again. "Kate, you'd need more trees than we have on our thousand-acre property."

"Ouch! That's a little harsh, don't you think?"

"I think what you just did to that poor tree is harsh. It doesn't even look like a tree anymore. All of the others are going to make fun of it."

"So your trees not only have names, but feelings, too?" Kate mocked with a pop of just one eyebrow. "What is this, some sort of magical Christmas tree farm?"

"Something like it."

Taking one of his leather work gloves into his hand, Deacon moved closer and dusted it across Kate's shoulder. A few pine needles shook loose but the good majority remained stuck to her like Velcro. "You're a mess. For someone who spends so much time in front of the camera, I figured you'd care a little more about your appearance."

"What I care about is doing a good job. Plus, you've made it clear that my camera isn't really welcome here. Who am I trying to impress?"

Deacon didn't offer an answer for that. "I've got another task I think you might be better at. I'll have Cody finish up for us here." Nudging his chin, Deacon motioned for Kate to follow. "Let's head to the storage barn and I'll show you what's next on the agenda for today."

"Does it involve wearing boots? Because my feet are killing me and I'm dying to get these things off my feet."

"Weren't you wearing high heels yesterday?"

"My feet are trained for heels. But these boots?" She lifted one foot from the ground and dropped it back down into the snow. "These are the most uncomfortable shoes I've ever squished my feet into."

There was that laugh again, so unexpected it made Kate falter. "You just need to break them in."

"And how long does that take?"

"To get them to the point where they mold to your feet? Roughly a hundred hours of wear."

Kate snorted. "Oh, is that all?"

"You know, I actually slept in my first pair of cowboy boots. Granted, I was five and had asked for a real pair for two Christmases running. Don't think my mom could've pried them from my feet with a crowbar if she'd wanted to. I loved those boots," Deacon said almost longingly as he relayed the sweet memory. "But that's always an option."

"Might not be a bad idea. Then I'll be prepared to

stomp all the spiders that crawl across the floor in the middle of the night. It's a win-win."

Deacon halted in his tracks. A concerned expression marred his face. "There are spiders in the loft?"

"Well, I haven't technically seen a spider yet, but the abundance of cobwebs makes me think they're not too far off. Where there's smoke there's fire sort of thing and all."

"That's no good. I'm sorry about that, Kate." With his large hand, he rubbed the back of his neck as though almost embarrassed by the news. "I can get those cleaned up for you."

"It's really not a problem. I can handle bugs. You know, I once spent some time in pest management."

"Yeah, I saw that piece—" Deacon cut himself off before Kate had the chance to.

"Deacon Winters, did you look me up?"

"I do background checks on all of my employees."

She knew it was an attempt to backpedal but she couldn't let him off that easily. "Sure, but that story was *way* deep in the archives. Like my first year doing *On the Job*."

"Really? It was the first thing that popped up for me."

That wasn't true. Kate was well aware that her most-watched segment was the one of her time as an exotic cat tamer. It was the first link on the first page of a simple internet search. She couldn't fathom why Deacon would lie about it, but she'd already made him feel bad about the spiders. And after overhearing his conversation with his mother earlier that morning, Kate figured she should cut Deacon a little slack. It was clear he was going through something private and she would respect that.

The rest of the walk was quiet, save for the crunching of packed snow under the tread of their shoes. As they trekked through the magnificently tall pines, Kate drew in an expansive breath, treasuring the mountain air that seemed to cleanse not only her lungs, but her head, too. She'd come to terms with the new way she had to complete this assignment. She'd even come to terms with the grumpy tree farmer she'd be working alongside. If there was one thing she had learned over the years as a reporter, it was how to catch a curve ball.

But the bigger curve ball here was the way she found herself admiring Deacon while they walked side by side through his family's tree farm. He was a tall man, his stature strikingly broad and commanding. Even though he kept them shaded under the brim of a white cowboy hat, she could see he had warm, chestnut-colored eyes rimmed with a fringe of dark lashes. There was a permanent stubble spread across his angular jaw, like he didn't own a razor capable of shaving it clean. Every bit of Deacon was masculine, from his mussed hair kept slightly too long down to his broken-in boots.

Kate worked with attractive men, that was a given. Many of the television reporters at her station had faces that were classically handsome. But what she never found attractive was the amount of time—and sometimes even makeup—necessary to make them appear that way. Deacon, on the other hand, had a ruggedly natural appeal that caught her completely off-guard. Even more so when he looked at her the way he was at that very moment.

"What?" she said, instantly self conscious. His eyes felt heavy on her like a physical touch and her heart rate dialed up several notches.

"Nothing." He shrugged. "It's just that I think I might owe you an apology."

"Really?" A laugh flew from Kate's mouth. "I figured I'd have to wait more than a day to get one of those from you."

"So you do agree that I owe you one?"

It was Kate's turn to shrug. "I mean, you were a little rude to me yesterday."

"I was. And I'm sorry for that," he readily admitted, surprising her yet again. "I'm still irritated that my mother didn't fill me in on everything. But that's not your fault, so I apologize for second-guessing your abilities. I did spend some time watching your show, Kate. You really don't shy away from the hard stuff and that's an admirable quality."

She didn't have a mirror to confirm it, but Kate could sense her cheeks had turned tomato red based on the heat of them alone. She hadn't expected that small bit of praise from the gruff cowboy. "Well, I appreciate that. I might not always be a rock star at these new jobs, but I'm sure gonna give it my all."

"Yeah, I think you gave that poor tree your all and then some."

"I really did butcher it, didn't I?"

"I didn't think it could get worse than a Charlie

Brown tree, to be honest. But a Kate Carmichael tree might take the cake."

They made amiable small talk the rest of the way to the barn and once they reached it, Deacon held the door open to allow Kate through first. Even underneath many layers of winter clothes, his hand lighting on the small of her back made a shiver zoom up her spine.

"How many barns do you have?" Kate wondered aloud as Deacon guided them toward a large metal desk with two folding chairs, one placed on either side. There was a rusty green tractor parked in the center of the metal dwelling, several wooden Christmas-themed cutouts tilted like leaning dominoes and a handful of sawhorses and other classic farm tools.

"We've just got this storage barn and then the barn you're staying in where we keep the animals. We do most of our work from here."

"And you live on the property?"

"I do. Just up near the road. I built myself a little place a few years back. Nothing special, but it's enough for me."

"And your mom and Cody live in the main house?"

"Yep."

Kate wanted to know more about the Winters family. She could feel the decades of tradition on the farm but she figured that was a conversation for later. At the present time, all she cared to do was redeem herself after that awful pruning snafu.

Deacon dropped into a chair and pulled a binder from the desk drawer, then slid it across the table. "We'll be starting our rental tree deliveries this week, but we need to call all of our customers first to see what day works best for them for drop-offs. I'll take A through M, you take N through Z. I don't like to schedule more than a dozen deliveries a day, so we'll keep track on this paper." He placed a lined sheet on the surface between them. "You comfortable with that or would you rather I find you something else to work on?"

Kate beamed. "I talk for a living, Deacon. This is right up my alley."

DEACON

The woman wasn't kidding. Kate Carmichael sure had the gift of gab. Deacon had completed his list of phone calls in a quarter the time it took her to finish her call log. For Deacon, all it boiled down to was a simple, "Hello, Deacon Winters here from Yuletide Tree Farm. We have your rental tree ready for delivery next week. What day works best?" followed by a one-word answer.

Not so for Kate.

He'd timed one of her phone calls: nine minutes and forty-three seconds. He didn't bother clocking any others after that for fear the battery on his watch would completely drain. From what he could overhear, she'd been promised a free cup of coffee from Mrs. Carlton whose family ran *The Bossy Bean* in town. The Hastings had invited her to church the following weekend. She'd convinced Tamara Miraz to commit to dyeing her hair fire engine red, something the woman had apparently contemplated for over six months but had yet to pull the trigger on.

And he was pretty sure Tanner Blightly, the local high school's football coach, had asked her out on a date during the last phone call.

Deacon couldn't explain it, but that proposal didn't sit well with him.

When she hung up the phone for the final time, Kate blew out a breath that lifted her wheat-blonde hair from her face.

"Whew!" She melted into the chair as she leaned back, no doubt worn out from the hours of chitchat. That much talk certainly would've exhausted Deacon. "Your customers are great. So personable. And they all agree you have the best trees around. Every single person sang your farm's praises."

"I'm a little surprised they were able to get a word in," he said with a friendly smirk.

"You don't think I talked too much, do you? I've been told I tend to do that."

"Not at all. It sounded like every customer was quite willing and eager to chat with you."

That answer seemed to appease her as the smile that had momentarily fallen from her mouth returned. "You're already done with your list?"

"Have been for some time."

"Not much of a talker, are you, Deacon Winters?"

He maneuvered around the question without completely answering it. "I'm talking to you now, aren't I?"

"Only because I asked you a question. But I get the

sense you're not really one to volunteer information without being directly asked for a response. Is that the case?"

"Is this another question?"

"Might be."

Deacon thought on it for a brief moment. "I don't see the point in volunteering more information than necessary."

"What do you consider necessary?" Kate's fingers wove together as she clasped her hands in front of her on the metal table separating them. It was the first time Deacon had given them any real notice. He couldn't help the strange sense of relief that swelled within him when he confirmed her fourth finger was ring-free.

"What's necessary?" He yanked his gaze from her hands and directed it back up to her eyes, the sparkling blue that made his breath catch. Even if her words didn't push him for an answer, the look of expectation set on her face more than encouraged one. "I don't know. Name. Occupation. Stuff like that."

"So all your customers know about you is that your name is Deacon Winters and you sell Christmas trees?"

"That pretty much sums me up."

"Oh Deacon, I have a feeling there's a lot more to discover under that burly exterior."

His chin tugged back. "Did you just call me burly?"

"Well, yeah." Kate pinned her full bottom lip between her teeth as she stifled a giggle. "You are pretty much the epitome of a mountain man."

"That's what you think I am?" He half-laughed. "Just some mountain man?"

"Do you want to give me more to work with?"

At that very moment, a dawning of understanding jolted through Deacon like the sharp pang of indigestion after a spicy meal. He grimaced at the sick feeling that snaked through his gut. "I'm not really up for being interviewed, Kate."

"That's not what I was doing."

"Maybe not, but that's what it feels like. It feels like you're trying to pull information out of me that I don't want to give."

"I'm sorry if it feels that way, Deacon. It's certainly not my intent. I just asked if there's more to you than being a tree farmer."

"There's not."

With the most nonchalantly aggravating little shrug, she said, "Well, there's more to me than my profession. I'm a Leo. A champion spelling bee winner and avid knitter. In fact, I made this scarf. I can make you one, if you like."

"That's not necessary."

"I'm just trying to make a point. You can pretend you're one-dimensional, but we're not paper dolls, Deacon. We all have feelings. Hopes and dreams."

"I think we're about done here."

Kate took a fortifying breath. "You do realize this is the second day in a row you've cut the workday short because I said something you didn't want to hear, right?"

He wasn't doing that. Was he? "We've checked everything off today's list."

She met and held his gaze like a standoff. "Sure,

we have."

"I'm beginning to think it should be called *On the Spot* instead of *On the Job*."

"I'm sorry if I've put you on the spot. I really am," she said with a sincerity that couldn't be ignored. "I'm just inquisitive by nature and sometimes it doesn't occur to me that that can potentially make people uncomfortable. I'll try to be more aware of it from here on out."

Kate's quick acquiescence made a sliver of guilt snag in Deacon's stomach. Why was he trying to pick a fight with this woman? She didn't deserve it, even if her poking and prodding into his personal life made him feel vulnerable in a way he hadn't been in years.

"Listen, I think I'm just tired and maybe I'm taking that out on you. I didn't sleep well. Sometimes that makes me short-tempered."

"Is that it? Because I thought maybe you were hangry."

"Yeah. A bit of that, too, I suppose," Deacon acknowledged, grateful for the levity in their suddenly strained conversation. "How about we fix that and head into town to grab some dinner? There's a great spot that I'm confident you'll like. It's a local favorite." He stretched out a hand like an offering.

"Do we get to talk during this dinner?" Kate asked. Her hand stilled between them, not quite willing to commit to the handshake yet. "Or do I have to stay quiet?"

"I'll answer three questions, so choose them wisely."

With a laugh and a smile, Kate shoved her hand into his. "Deal."

KATE

"I love this song!" Kate lunged across the console and took hold of the radio dial to crank up the volume. Bing Crosby's mellow baritone filled the cab of Deacon's truck with tunes of holiday joy that were as warm as her favorite knit sweater. She slumped back against the seat and melted into that feeling, allowing the notes and the melody to wash over her with gladness. "What's your favorite Christmas carol?"

They had opted to drive to dinner together. That was a relief Kate didn't make known vocally, but felt all the same in the noticeable relaxation of her shoulders the moment Deacon offered to take the helm. Her little sedan didn't have the knobby snow tires that his pickup sported, and she'd absentmindedly left the newly purchased chains required for these sorts of conditions back at her downtown apartment. Plus, she didn't know the first thing about driving on sleet or snow-covered roads. With her luck, she'd either fishtail the entire way to the diner or end up stranded in an icy embankment, the sorts of winter accidents her counterparts at the station reported on all season long. Best to leave it to the expert in this particular scenario.

"You sure you want to use one of your questions on that?" Deacon asked.

"You can learn a lot about someone by their song choice. It's a valid question."

Eyes forward, Deacon's mouth hooked up on one side. "How about I let you guess?"

"Oh!" Kate perked up and wriggled in her seat, excited at that option. "I like that. Make a game of it. Okay."

She adjusted her seatbelt strap, really getting comfortable as she sized up the man next to her. He had pulled his signature white hat from his head, leaving it to rest on the dashboard below. His profile was strong, much like his presence. At first glance, Deacon seemed like a what-you-see-is-what-you-get sort of man, but their limited interactions had already demonstrated otherwise. There were layers under that exterior. Kate was sure of it. And she was determined to peel them back.

"*Twelve Days of Christmas*?" she posited after thinking on it for over a mile's worth of silence.

"Really?" A bellow of laughter let her know she'd struck out. "There are a whole lot more than twelve days of Christmas when you run a tree farm. More like three-hundred-sixty-five. Guess again."

"I want to say something goofy like *Rockin' Around the Christmas Tree*, but that feels too obvious. Plus, you've got far too many trees to rock around. You'd get dizzy. And I don't take you for much of a dancer."

"I'll have you know I'm a *great* dancer," he defended, slapping a palm to the steering wheel as he let out a hoot of pure delight. "You're looking at our high school's senior class square-dancing champion in P.E."

"Is it possible that you just volunteered information about yourself without me having to pull it from you?"

Screwing up his mouth into a pout, he snorted. "Only because that title is absolutely brag-worthy."

"I'll give you that," Kate played along because it was too fun not to. "It really is."

"One more guess."

"And if I don't get it?"

"Then I suppose you'll never know."

Kate grinned. "Then I'm going to wait until I'm really confident."

Pulling up to their destination, Deacon angled his truck into the entrance of a dimly lit parking lot. A log structure that looked similar to the ones Kate used to make with building blocks as a child rested on the other side of the pavement. The backdrop of snow-tipped trees made the restaurant feel like a natural part of its surroundings, almost as though it had always been a piece of the landscape. Icicles clung to the building's peaks and gutters were strung with colorful lights that flashed like beacons of holiday cheer. It was the most welcoming sight, both to her heart and to her growling stomach.

"This is the place," Deacon noted as he tugged his

keys out of the ignition. The engine hissed quietly under the hood. "I hope you're hungry."

"I could eat a horse," Kate exclaimed, unhooking her lapbelt and letting it fly.

"I'll be sure not to repeat that information to Sarge."

Deacon hopped down from his truck and closed his door into place behind him. Before Kate could move her fingers to her own door handle, Deacon was standing at her side of the vehicle.

"Careful." He opened the door for her, letting a blast of icy air swirl into the cab and he surprised her again when he took her hand. "The running boards tend to get slick."

She had no desire to end up on her backside in front of this man for a second time in two short days, so she readily grasped onto his proffered hand. "Thank you. I appreciate it."

Side by side, they huddled against the cold, their paces quickening as they scurried up the slushy stone path toward the entrance. There was a set of outdoor speakers hanging under the eaves and the up-tempo carol, *We Wish You a Merry Christmas*, met their ears like a formal holiday greeting. Kate's thoughts spun back to Christmases past, to the many spent alone in her small apartment with a lukewarm take out meal and a glass of celebratory champagne for one. She'd never minded the solitude. Not entirely, at least. Due to the nature of her job, so much of her life was spent in the company of others. Of course, as a true extrovert, Kate adored that aspect of things, but she also understood Christmastime was meant for family.

Inside the restaurant was crowded, living up to Deacon's assertion that it was indeed a local favorite. The lobby teemed with customers congregating around a massive stone fireplace that donned colorful knit stockings in festive greens and reds. Across the lobby, there was a stately tree wedged in the corner bearing ball ornaments with names of the restaurant's employees penned in glittering gold, and cranberry garland coiled up the evergreen like train tracks twisting up a steep mountain. It was everything Kate imagined a Sierra dining establishment to be: cozy, familiar, and much to her relief, overwhelmingly warm.

They sat on a wooden bench made for four, but due to the crowd it currently held twice that amount. She couldn't turn to look at Deacon without feeling intimately close, like they were both invading one another's personal bubble by at least two feet. Kate flipped a menu over, busying her hands and eyes so she didn't focus on the way her leg lined up next to Deacon's or how their elbows touched with every slight movement or jostle. "What do you usually get?"

"Prime rib. Twice baked potato. Green beans. Slice of chocolate cake."

"Every time?"

"Every time."

"Where's the adventure in that?" Kate lowered the menu to her lap and chanced a look up at Deacon right when he happened to do the same. As their gazes met, she felt their proximity as a low flutter in her stomach, like the release of a butterfly swarm. She forced a swallow that bordered on a gulp and prayed Deacon was illiterate when it came to reading body language.

"You saw those driving conditions, right?" he asked, almost rhetorically. He nodded toward the window that framed in the landscape like a wintery, nostalgic painting and cocked his head slightly. "It's an adventure out on those roadways all season long. I don't want an adventure when it comes to my food, too. Some things need to be consistent in life and I, for one, think food should be that way."

"You do make a fair point. I'll give you that."

"Deacon, party of two!" the hostess behind the podium interrupted their conversation and it couldn't have come at a better time. Each minute spent squeezed up against Deacon's big body made Kate feel increasingly out of sorts. She welcomed a table's distance between them. It was as though her thoughts had come completely unraveled and she needed some space to spool them back up and pull herself together.

"Nice to see you, Deacon." The young hostess flashed a genial smile over her shoulder while the trio maneuvered around the tables and chairs spaced throughout the restaurant. There really wasn't an empty table in sight as families and friends all had the same idea to gather and share an evening meal.

"Same to you, Sarah. How's the family?"

"Everyone's doing well. The boys are excited to come on out to the farm and cut down their tree next week. It's all they've been talking about."

"Well, we do have one or two for them to choose

from," Deacon noted with the touch of sarcasm Kate had come to expect.

As promised, the woman showed them to their table and if Kate had been flustered by their closeness on the bench in the lobby, this setup wasn't going to alleviate that. The booth had high back, leather seat cushions, bolstered on the ends with upright, rustic logs that stretched all the way to the A-frame ceiling. This portion of the establishment was secluded and the flickering tea light candles centered on the table screamed date night. Despite the many people in the building, this particular table was meant for privacy.

"Will this do?"

"Yeah, this should be fine," Deacon answered for them.

"Good." The hostess deposited two menus onto the table and stepped back, hands folded. "Because it's the only available one we've got. I'll leave you both to get settled in. Tommy should be by shortly to take your order. Enjoy your dinner."

"Thank you." Kate unbuttoned her jacket and placed it onto the seat cushion before sliding in next to it.

Pressing his shirt to his stomach, Deacon lowered into his side, wiggling in. Kate could instantly see how tightly he wedged into the narrow booth, almost too big to fit.

"Do you want to wait until one of the other tables opens up?" Kate offered. "Might give us a little more room. I'm totally fine with waiting."

"Nope." He removed his hat. "I'm too hungry. This'll work."

"But you look uncomfortable."

With two hands gripping the table's ledge, Deacon slid the solid wood fixture a few inches closer toward Kate. Even still, she had ample room.

"I'm good now," he said as he stretched out, arms splayed wide as he rested them on the back of his cushion. "We make a good pair."

She knew he referred to his large size and her small stature, but she couldn't keep her mind from traveling into territory it had no business entering. They weren't a couple in that way. They were like oil and water. Cats and dogs. Total opposites in every area. That was a recipe for relationship disaster.

"What are you thinking?" he said, collecting a menu she figured he already had memorized.

"That you and I would never work."

Deacon sputtered a cough. "I meant, what are you thinking for dinner?"

This is where Kate wished she could cut to commercial. Someone was going to need to script her conversations if she let stupid things like that fall from her lips. "Oh. Of course. Right. Dinner."

"But I'd like to hear more about this—"

"I misunderstood you." She threw her menu up in front of her face like a paper barricade. "The roasted chicken looks good. Salmon, too."

"What do you mean, we would never work?"

"I saw someone with the chicken pot pie when we walked in. I haven't had one of those in years. I don't like peas though, and it says here they put peas in theirs. Maybe I'll be able to pick them out. What do you think?"

When Deacon's index finger hooked over the top of her menu and lowered it, revealing his smirking face on the other side, she wanted to crawl under the table. "Why wouldn't we work, Kate?"

She let the menu flutter down between them. "Well, for starters, we can't even *work* together in a professional capacity. Working in a relationship would be even more disastrous. Plus, you're not really my type."

"Your type isn't tall, dark—"

"And handsome?"

"You said it. Not me." Deacon shrugged so indifferently it had Kate wondering where this suddenly flirtatious version came from. This manifestation was certainly a new side of him. "So, what *is* your type?"

"I prefer men that don't make me feel small."

"I can't help that I'm six-four. I've always been sorta big. Even as a baby. I hold the record for the biggest one born at our local hospital, I'll have you know. Eleven pounds, thirteen ounces." He crossed his feet at the ankles and accidentally kicked Kate's shin under the table in the process. "Sorry."

"It's fine." She waved him off. "But I meant that I prefer men who don't make me feel small confidence-wise."

That comment appeared to hit Deacon with the force of a sledgehammer. He practically looked like he might become sick as his hand went to his stomach and clutched the fabric of his flannel shirt. "Is that how I make you feel?"

"In all honesty? A little. I can't blame it all on you, though. My boss had already taken me out at the knees with this whole assignment. I was supposed to have my cameraman with me, but at the last minute, she moved him over to another piece. My confidence was already rattled before I even got here. You just added to it."

Deacon's eyes found Kate's and an apologetic gaze swept over his strong features, molding them into something that had Kate losing her breath. "I can't say I'm not relieved that there's not a cameraman following us around since I wasn't even super thrilled with the idea of you filming with just your camera phone. But I had no idea I made you feel like you weren't capable, Kate. That's not how I feel. Quite the opposite, actually, now that I've seen your show. You're more than capable."

"Sure, but only if I have some material to work with," she replied with a hopeless shrug as she picked her menu back up.

"Then it's a good thing you've still got two more questions."

Tommy, the waiter Sarah had promised from earlier, ultimately arrived at the side of their table fifteen minutes later, out of breath with dark hair matted in sweat and an apron haphazardly tied around his middle. Everything about his demeanor indicated it had already been a rough night.

Yeah. I know the feeling, buddy, Deacon mused to himself.

His conversation with Kate had taken a swift and jerky turn. Not that it surprised him. Their discussions always seemed to do that. One minute things were civil —flirtatious, even—and then they were U-turning into downright uncomfortable territory. But learning he'd made her question her abilities was news Deacon never wanted to hear. He'd have to make that right.

"I'm so sorry," the waiter apologized as he pulled a pen and paper from his back pocket and scribbled circles onto the pad to get the ink flowing. "We're really slammed. Didn't mean to keep you waiting. My name's Tommy and I'll be helping you both out tonight. Would you like to hear our specials or do you already know what you'd like to order?"

Like the opposites they'd already proven to be, Kate answered that she'd love to hear the specials at the same time Deacon said it wouldn't be necessary, making their words jumble together like alphabet soup. That brought on a laugh from all parties, a welcome release that eased some of the tension mounting from earlier. They'd needed that.

While Tommy rattled off the dishes, Deacon found himself staring at the woman across the table. She was engaging in the way she made each person feel like the only one in the room. Even now, she hung on every word Tommy recited like he was telling her the secrets of the universe and not merely listing dinner entrees. Deacon honestly believed her interest wasn't fake or for show. Kate was the type of woman who cared about the intricate details of a person. She wanted to know what made them tick. What filled them with passion. With hope.

Deacon liked to give people their space, mostly because he valued his own. He'd made the mistake of letting someone in once and it left him exposed in a way he still hadn't fully recovered from.

"The half chicken," Kate said decisively, about to hand off the menu to Tommy. She yanked it back suddenly. "Actually, no. The short ribs. Yep. Let's go with the short ribs."

"One order of short ribs. Good choice," Tommy

said. He jotted her order into his notebook and turned to Deacon. "And for you?"

"Prime rib. Medium rare. Twice baked potato. Green beans."

"Great." The waiter clicked the end of his retractable pen and shoved it behind his ear. "We'll have those out for you in a bit. I'll send someone over with fresh bread, too."

Once Tommy retreated to the kitchen, Kate dragged the back of her hand across her brow with flair. "Whew! That was tough. Everything looks so delicious when you're hungry."

"I agree. That's why I only go grocery shopping after I've had a solid meal. I once bought two cartfuls of groceries I didn't really need because my stomach growled each time I turned down a new aisle."

"I've done that, too. The worst is when they have those little old ladies with the free samples. I end up buying everything they offer! I have no self control."

Kate laughed at herself as she reached for the bread basket that a busboy had recently left at their table just as Deacon made the same move. Their knuckles brushed. Deacon pulled back.

"You go ahead." He nodded toward the steaming pile of buttery rolls.

Conversations swelled around them but all Deacon could zero in on was Kate and the way she chewed and savored her food like it was her last meal. She made little sounds of delight with each bite popped into her mouth. "This bread is delicious."

"Pretty good, huh?"

"Better than the freezer meals I usually have."

"And you haven't even tasted the entrée yet." Deacon waited until she took her second roll before reaching into the basket for one of his own. "You really eat frozen dinners? I didn't realize people actually bought those."

"It's either that or takeout. I don't often have a lot of time to spend in the kitchen. Don't get me wrong because I absolutely love what I do, but it's a real struggle to find balance."

"I can imagine." Deacon aimed his eyes at Kate. "Alright. I'm ready."

"For what?" She held a bite-sized piece of bread up to her lips and gave him a funny look.

"For question number two."

"Oh! I had almost forgotten!"

Deacon shook his head. "No, you hadn't."

"You're right. I hadn't." She set the bread down and rubbed her hands together like she was revving up for something great. "Okay. Here it is. Question numero dos. Will you ever agree to a real interview with me? Like filmed and all? Something I can use for my show."

"That question only requires a one-word answer. Don't you want to ask something that will give you a little more to work with?"

"The answer to that question will give me *everything* to work with, Deacon," she said with conviction. "So what will it be? Yes?" Kate produced a massive grin. "Or no?" Her mouth overturned into a frown like she was the real life version of the comedy and tragedy theater masks.

"It's a yes."

"No way!" He wasn't prepared for the roll that launched out of her hand, smacking him squarely in the chest. "Oh my gosh! I'm so sorry! I didn't mean to throw that at you. You just got me a little excited."

"No worries." He took the bread from his lap and placed it onto his appetizer plate.

"You ready for question number three?"

"Am I going to need a catcher's glove for this reaction, too?"

"I promise I won't throw any more food at you." Kate made a little X under her collarbone with her pointer finger. "Cross my heart."

"Go for it."

She beamed. "Can this interview take place tomorrow when we're out delivering trees? I really want to get that on camera. I think the whole process will fascinate viewers. It's exactly the sort of thing to usher in the holiday season and get people excited about coming out to your farm to take a look at your trees."

"Another one-worder?"

"If I get an answer to this, then I can start planning how I'm going to tackle this whole assignment. I like to know what I'm getting myself into."

"And I'm a little worried about what I might be getting myself into."

Kate fluttered a dismissive hand. "I promise I won't ask you anything that will embarrass you or make your grandmother blush."

"Well, I wasn't concerned about that before, but now I am."

When Tommy finally returned with their dinner entrées, Kate and Deacon had fallen into a cadence of easy conversation. Deacon found himself almost disappointed by the interruption of food. He couldn't recall the last time he'd shared a meal with a woman like Kate. Or any woman, for that matter. Of course, this wasn't a date, but had it been, he would've found himself itching for a second one.

That thought made him nearly flinch.

"You okay?" Somehow, even from across the table, Kate noticed his small, jerky movement.

"Just bit my tongue," he lied. "You like the short ribs?"

"They are everything I hoped and dreamed they would be," she said with a smack of her lips.

Deacon didn't sense she was being facetious. Kate had big emotions. This was made very clear in the two short days he'd known her and while it originally frustrated him, he'd come to anticipate these big, exaggerated displays. Hope for them, even.

"How's your prime rib?"

"I do believe you've used up all of your questions for the night." He pointed the tines of his fork at her and made a *tsk*-ing sound.

"Oh, you're right." She played right along. "And I was going to ask you if maybe we could come back here again while I'm in town. I guess I'll have to find someone else to take me."

"I'll bring you back here." Deacon said it so quickly it made Kate's eyes round. That came across more forward than he had intended.

"I can write it off as a business expense," Kate suggested. "Put it on the company card and everything."

"That's not the way I work. I'll be paying."

"Seriously, Deacon, the station will pay for it."

Deacon tossed his napkin to his lap. "You're a woman. I'm a man. We're sharing a meal together and I intend on paying for it. Insist, even."

He swore he saw the faintest shade of pink paint Kate's cheeks and he hoped it was out of flattery and not embarrassment. She quickly squelched any worry he had over misspeaking when she said, "I can't remember the last time a man paid for my meal. Thank you, Deacon. I really do appreciate it. That's very generous of you."

"It won't be the last time," he said, hoping he wasn't being too forward again when he added, "No freezer meals for Kate Carmichael on my watch."

The sparkle in her eye and the growing upturn of her mouth was the only answer he needed.

KATE

"Knock, knock."

An insistent rapping against the barn loft door had Kate leaping out from under the cozy confines of her covers. She'd slept hard. The full meal likely had a little something to do with that. The fact that she hadn't been able to turn her brain off until after midnight probably contributed even more. Conversations replayed in her head like a looped musical track. It had been such a nice evening, one of the most enjoyable she'd had in recent days, and she didn't want the night to end, even in her thoughts.

"It's just me, dear," a woman's voice echoed when Kate had yet to respond. "Marla."

With a quick tug of a sweatshirt over her head, Kate padded the few steps to the door and opened it wide. "Morning, Marla. I hope Deacon relayed the memo that I wouldn't be joining you all for breakfast. I knew I'd still be full from last night's meal." She rubbed her satisfied belly.

"No worries, sweetie. We did a grab-and-go sort of thing this morning, anyway. But I thought you could hang onto this for a snack for later." She lobbed an orange at Kate like it was a softball and even though Kate admittedly lacked athletic dexterity, she managed to catch it one-handed. "And this came for you yesterday. Wanted to make sure you got it."

In Marla's other hand was a wrapped, brown paper package with a shipping label bearing Kate's name. "Not to be nosey or anything, but it's from someone named Toby. Boyfriend?"

That particular word made Kate balk. "Boyfriend? Goodness, no. Toby's my cameraman."

Something about that answer seemed to please the woman. "Understood. Anyway, the boys are just about done loading up the trees for today's deliveries. Deacon said you'd be busy with him all day, but I was hoping I could put in a request to reserve you for tomorrow. I need to make a dozen more wreaths before we open up our little farmstand shop and I could sure use another set of hands."

"I would love that," Kate started to say. "But I do have to warn you—"

"Already been warned." Marla lifted a hand like a pause button on Kate's confession. "Deacon mentioned pruning isn't really your thing. That's not a problem at all. I'll have all the sprigs cut and ready for assembly. You'll just have to attach them and add an embellishment here or there. Can't botch it. Completely foolproof."

Kate was a little surprised to learn Deacon had been talking about her—to his mother of all people. "Then I'm looking forward to it."

"Same, sweetie." Marla stepped over the threshold and squeezed Kate's shoulders, tugging her close for a brief hug before releasing her. Then she gave her a playful swat on her arm. "Now go on and get ready so you can finally get that interview of yours."

"Deacon told you he agreed to give me one?"

"He did. You know, Kate—Deacon is an obstinate man, there's no denying that. But he's not an unreasonable one. I think once he realized you were harmless, he saw no sense in digging in his heels just for stubbornness's sake," Marla explained, shedding some light on her son. "Like most men, he also does better when things are his idea." She gave Kate a wink. "Or at least when *he thinks* things are his idea."

"Appreciate the insight," Kate said. "And thank you for bringing this up for me." She shook the small package in her hands. "Even as an adult, it's always fun to get mail."

After Marla left, Kate readied for the day quickly. She decided on her favorite plaid flannel tucked neatly into dark denim jeans, topped off with a flashy studded belt she'd purchased the summer before at a cute, little western store in Old Sacramento. It took her almost twice as long to wedge her feet into her stiff cowgirl boots as it did to completely dress for the day. She wasn't sure she'd ever break those dang things in.

She had saved the package until now, loving the anticipation of a waiting gift and wishing to hang onto that sensation just a bit longer. Years back, Kate took a short online quiz to discover her love language. It came as no surprise that gift giving—and in turn, receiving— was right at the top. She relished the glow of appreciation on a loved one's face when opening a present selected just for them. Toby knew that, and her heart swelled at the fact that he'd remembered her in this way.

She tore into the package with gusto, only stopping to read the little note resting atop a pile of foam packing peanuts.

Figured this might help you out a little. You've got this, Kate! Go get 'em!

Smiling, she set the notecard aside and thrust her fingers into the package to root around for the gift.

"A selfie stick?" she pondered aloud once her hands landed on the object and pulled it free. She couldn't hold back a chuckle. Never in her life did she think she'd own one of these silly contraptions. She couldn't say it wouldn't be helpful, though. Snagging her cell phone from the nightstand, Kate clipped it to the device, extended the rod, and tested it out, fixing on her widest grin and giving an enthusiastic thumbs-up to the camera. Retracting the long arm, she fired off the picture in a text to her long-time friend.

Just what I needed! Thank you for thinking of me, Toby! It's perfect.

Within seconds, her cameraman's reply of a smiley face emoji popped onto her phone screen, making Kate beam.

She gathered her tote bag, threw the stick inside, and locked up the loft. Bella and Sarge nickered as she descended the squeaky barn stairs. They lifted their heads to snort a morning greeting with bits of hay poking out from their large muzzles. As Kate shuffled by, she struggled to keep from wincing. If her feet were already giving her this much grief only five minutes into her morning, she couldn't fathom the shape they'd be in come evening time.

"Hey there, horses," she acknowledged each animal with a grin and a pat on the cheek. "Enjoying your breakfast?"

Practically tiptoeing, Kate continued up the barn aisle. The low hum of Deacon's truck motor—followed by the squealing of the unoiled trailer lagging behind as it hauled a thick cluster of rental Christmas trees—was a welcome, appreciated sound. The only prescription for Kate's current discomfort was to get off her feet as quickly as possible.

Deacon left the vehicle idling and jogged up. "Good morning, Kate."

"Morning, Deacon."

"I see you dropped the 'good' part." His gaze landed on her feet, almost as though he could read her mind— or more accurately, her pain. "Boots still bothering you?"

"Oh, you know. Only ninety-five more hours and I'll be just fine."

He thumbed his chin right in the middle where Kate noticed a small divot that she hadn't detected before. "You probably wear…what? A seven?"

"Wow. That's impressive. You have some women's footwear fetish I should know about?"

Deacon rolled his eyes. "Hang tight. I think I might have a solution." With that, he disappeared into a room off the side of the barn that had a wooden sign with the word *Tack* nailed above it. She could hear him rustling around for a moment, and when he finally returned, he had a beautifully broken in pair of boots in his hand and a hopeful grin on his face. "Think these will work?"

"Give me those!" Kate made grabby hands. She tugged the boots free and plopped to the ground right where she stood to swap out the torture devices currently on her feet.

"You're not weirded out by wearing someone else's shoes?"

"You obviously didn't see the *On the Job* episode where I disinfected shoes at the local bowling alley. Not much grosses me out, Deacon."

"You're certainly full of surprises," he said, almost in passing. He clamped his hands together. "Ready to get started?"

"With the interview?" Kate's level of enthusiasm matched a child asked if they wanted a bowl of candy for breakfast.

"Well, I meant with our day, but I suppose that does involve an interview," Deacon acknowledged. "A promise is a promise."

"And I promise this won't be as painful as you think it will be." She reached into her tote bag and pulled out Toby's gift, excited to give it a whirl.

Deacon recoiled. "What in the world is that?"

"This?" She extended the arm of the device to full length which made Deacon withdraw even further. He was practically sandwiched against the barn wall, looking for escape. "It's a selfie stick."

"A whaty-what?"

"Oh, come on Deacon. You've heard of a selfie stick before."

"I haven't."

Kate gaped. "For real?"

"Yes, for real."

"It's a stick used for selfies."

Deacon shook his head. "What's a selfie?"

"Oh my word, Deacon, are you living under a Christmas tree? You've never heard of a selfie?"

His face remained devoid of any hint of comprehension.

"It's when you take a picture of yourself with your phone."

"Why would you take a picture of yourself with your phone?"

"I don't know. To post on social media. Like if you're traveling or eating out or at a concert or something. You take a picture of yourself and you post it."

"Why would anyone want to look at a picture of someone doing any of those things?"

"Oh Deacon, I can think of many, many women who wouldn't object to seeing your face while they scrolled through their social media feeds." Kate didn't think it possible, but Deacon's expression grew even more bewildered. "You *do* own a mirror, don't you?"

"How do the boots fit?" Deacon changed the subject

so fast she nearly felt the whiplash of his words. Kate had obviously made him uncomfortable, something she'd assured wouldn't happen during the interview. Great. She was off to a fantastic start.

Wriggling her toes, she answered, "The boots are perfect. Almost like they were made for me."

Just like her previous comment, this one also appeared to rattle Deacon. He spun around on his heel, made long, ground covering strides toward the truck and Kate made a mental note not to mention the boots again when he said, "Time to get on the road. These trees aren't going to deliver themselves."

DEACON

Kate's hand on Deacon's forearm made him pause, and not just because she was purposefully trying to halt him, which she was. What tripped him up was his reaction to it. A lump lodged squarely in his throat and he had an impossible time swallowing around it. Coughing wouldn't even clear it. This bizarre response was not unlike the shiver that skittered up his spine the night before; when their fingertips had brushed over the bread basket and he felt like he'd been shocked with a live Christmas light strand.

Before Deacon could waste any more time analyzing his almost laughable schoolboy reaction to Kate's touch, she whipped out that silly selfie stick and fixed it onto her phone.

"I want to get this on camera." She then ran her free hand over her golden hair to smooth down the flyaways and swiped her tongue over her front teeth. She must've picked up on the perplexed look on Deacon's face because she justified, "I've been caught on camera with lipstick on these pearly whites more times than I can count. Super unprofessional, not to mention embarrassing."

When she moved close and lifted a hand to adjust Deacon's skewed shirt collar, he trapped his breath in his lungs like a swimmer preparing for a heat. He knew his breaths trembled with this unanticipated closeness. Kate was an observant woman. She would easily pick up on the shakiness that paired with each inhale and exhale. For that reason, he figured the better option would be to pause breathing altogether.

"*Breathe*, Deacon." Yep, nothing got past Kate Carmichael. "No need to be nervous. If we don't like this take, we'll just do another."

"Sounds doable enough." Deacon messed with his wonky collar some more and leaned against the bumper of the trailer, arms threaded over his chest while he tried his best to appear cool. Collected. Two things that didn't even come close to describing the man at the present moment. "Ready whenever you are."

She flicked a finger over his shoulder. "Let's get one of the trees down and place it in between us. I think that will look nice and festive with the truck and trailer in the background holding the rest."

Deacon agreed and once they were situated with the Douglas fir in the center of the shot, Kate pressed her finger on the record button. "Good morning, Sacramento!" She smiled into the camera like she was talking to an old friend. "It's been an exciting couple days up here in the Sierras and as promised, I'm back to give you a little inside look at my current life as a Christmas tree farmer." She angled toward Deacon, motioning with her hand as an introduction. "I'm here today with Deacon Winters, the man in charge at Yuletide Tree Farm and we're just about to deliver our first rental tree of the season. If you haven't heard of living Christmas trees yet, get ready for that to be a new phrase in your holiday vocabulary. Actually, Deacon, would you mind explaining just what that is for our viewers?"

"I'd be happy to, Kate," Deacon replied. He coughed softly and nodded, readying to start in, but when he opened his mouth, no words followed.

"Can you tell us a little about the rental tree program you have for your customers at Yuletide Tree Farm?" Kate prompted.

Deacon was sure in any other scenario he could— he'd created the program, after all—but at that moment if someone had asked him his name, he wasn't positive he'd be able to provide them the correct answer. He was entirely mute.

Kate pulled the phone down. "It's just you and me, Deacon."

"And your twenty-thousand viewers."

"But they're not here right now." She placed the selfie stick on the trailer's bumper and collected Deacon's hands into her own. "We're just two friends having a conversation."

And holding hands, Deacon mused.

"There are no wrong answers," she encouraged. "Just speak from your heart."

"Since I couldn't even speak from my mouth, I don't think my heart will come any more naturally."

"Deacon? Deacon Winters?"

He couldn't have coordinated a better time for Blanche Cartwright to throw open her cherry red front door and descend down her walkway. Sweat had started to collect in his palms, and with his hands still in Kate's grip, there'd be no way to disguise that tell-tale sign of growing unease. He needed an out and at that moment, Blanche Cartwright was it.

"You're here with my tree!" The woman had her hands thrown skyward in praise. "I was just telling Bert that it isn't Christmastime until the Yuletide tree is up and trimmed. And here you are! Hallelujah!"

"Now *that* is a greeting," Kate murmured as their heads swiveled the direction of the emphatic customer bounding toward them. "I sure wish I had my camera rolling for that."

"Oh, Deacon!" Blanche clasped her hands near her bosom. "Is that one ours? She's just gorgeous! Look at those full branches. Even more beautiful than last year."

"Yes, ma'am. This is the one." Deacon bent to grab the tree's pot and hoisted the evergreen into his arms. "Where's she going? Same spot as last year?"

Blanche was about to answer when Kate cut in, a hand pushed into the space separating Deacon and the woman. "Hi there. I'm Kate Carmichael and I'm on assignment for Channel 14 News out of the valley. Would you mind terribly if I recorded your tree delivery today? I'm putting together a piece on Yuletide Tree Farm and I really think you'd be great on camera."

"You'd like to record me for television?" The woman looked aghast with disbelief.

"Yes, but only if you're comfortable—"

"Am I comfortable? Darling, I was made for the silver screen! The ladies down at church will never believe this! I've always told them I missed my calling as an actress. They tease me that I'm too much, even for Hollywood, but I know they're just giving me a hard time. Maybe even a little jealous." Blanche looked like she could spontaneously combust with joy. "What are my lines? I'm great at memorizing. Would you believe I can recite all the states' capitols in alphabetical order? Albany, New York. Annapolis, Maryland. Atlanta—"

"No memorized lines. I'll just film as Deacon carries your tree into the house and then I'll ask a few questions about your experience with the farm. Maybe get some footage of you hanging a few ornaments if that's okay."

"If that's okay?" Blanche grabbed Kate by the shoulders and shook her wildly like a hopeful child shaking a piggy bank. "This is the greatest thing to happen to me since I won pancakes for a year down at *The Toasty Tater*. Remember that, Deacon? Nine-hundred and sixty-four entries and I had the winning ticket."

"Sure do."

"I thought I'd used up all my life's luck on that, but then you come driving up with my tree, asking me to be on your show. Don't think I can handle much more excitement than this!"

Deacon looked directly at Kate when he said, "It's

definitely not everyday that you get to be interviewed by a reporter as prestigious as Kate Carmichael."

"It sure isn't. Oh, my stars. Bert's gonna fall over dead when I tell him."

Kate's eyes flashed. "Let's hope not—"

"Follow me on in, Deacon. The tree is going right in front of the big bay windows like always." With a swing of her hips, Blanche pivoted around and sauntered up the path with sashaying, wide movements fit for the catwalk. "Are we recording?"

Kate lifted her phone. "We are now."

If Kate hoped for a backdrop that could rival the North Pole, Blanche's home fit the bill and then some. This was always Deacon's favorite part of deliveries. He loved to see his neighbors' homes fully decked out for the holidays. Each house was different—the ornamentations, the smells, the extent to which they created a winter wonderland within their four walls. But the holiday comfort was the same. Christmas would always be Deacon's favorite time of year and he was grateful to have a job that celebrated it each and every day.

As he maneuvered around a huge Santa statue that came clear up to his shoulders, he could hear Kate recording an introduction for the interview. *Just a conversation between friends,* he replayed her words of encouragement in his mind. That likely came so naturally for Kate because she viewed everyone as a potential friend. Deacon wondered if that was innate or something learned over her many years in the business. There was a symbiotic relationship between a reporter and the interviewee and instant trust was a necessary element.

It surprised him how quickly he'd grown to trust Kate, and yet, he still knew so little about her.

"This is where that majestic tree goes!" Blanche took an over-the-top bow as she waved toward the only empty portion of floor space visible throughout the home. Every other surface was dusted with flocked snow and loaded with Christmas décor. Blanche was right, the tree was the only element left.

Deacon happily occupied himself with the setup while the women conversed at his back.

"And how many years has this particular rental tree had its holiday home at your place?" Kate asked.

"This is our fifth year, I believe. We were one of the first families to sign up for the rental program, if I remember correctly."

"And what led you to going the living tree route?"

"Well, we had been cutting down our trees at Yule-tide for years," Blanche explained, looking deeply into the camera as though auditioning for a feature film. "When our kids were still at home, it was such fun to load up in the car and head down to the farm. They loved roaming the forest and finding the perfect tree. Even fought over who got to chop it down. Deacon's trees are the best, but even great trees don't last forever once they are cut. Every year, when Christmas passed and the tree started to die, so did a little bit of my spirit."

Deacon prayed his snort wasn't picked up by Kate's phone. He thought Kate had a flair for the dramatic, but Blanche's antics were Oscar-worthy.

"I just hated putting that dry, brown thing out on the

street to be collected and thrown into a landfill," she elaborated. "Seemed so wasteful."

"So you were drawn to the idea of having a living tree instead?" Kate inferred.

"Absolutely. For us, it was the perfect solution. We get to have the same tree every year and we also feel like we're doing our part for the environment. It's become a tradition as important to us as Grandma Tilly's infamous fruitcake."

Deacon had sincerely hoped she'd forgotten, but when Blanche reached for a cardboard box resting on the fireplace mantel nearby, he realized he wouldn't be able to avoid the camera much longer.

"And my absolute favorite tradition is placing this star right at the tip-top." Blanche withdrew the glittering decoration from its storage place and held it expectantly. "The big bonus is that with a man like Deacon delivering our tree, there's no need to haul out the ladder. Sweetheart, would you be so kind as to help me out again this year?"

He'd wanted to get through this particular delivery without making his camera debut, but putting the topper on Blanche's tree was tradition and he wasn't going to let his nerves—or his pride—take that from her.

"I'd be honored." He hardly had to stretch to place the shiny, bright star right at the apex of the tree.

"Deck the halls!" Blanche shouted.

Kate pulled the camera close and said a few final words before clicking the screen and stowing it away. She had Blanche sign some sort of release which made the woman feel even more like a genuine superstar, and

Kate thanked her again for the opportunity before they were merrily on their way.

The next few deliveries followed the same pattern. Kate would introduce herself to an overjoyed customer who couldn't be happier than to oblige for an interview. Not a single one put up the stink Deacon had. That made him wonder if he'd made this entire interview process out to be something it wasn't. Still, he couldn't understand the whole fifteen-minutes-of-fame thing. If it were entirely up to him, he'd be happy with a lifetime of anonymity.

Somehow, he had a feeling he wouldn't have much say in that matter.

KATE

*L*et me know if you need anything else! I hope there's something here you can work with.

Kate composed and sent the text to Cora Langley, the IT expert down at the news station. She had just uploaded the day's footage to a shared online folder and finally felt her shoulders sag in sweet relief. Doing things this way wasn't altogether terrible. In fact, Kate enjoyed the freedom she had in capturing every aspect of the day from her own perspective.

With each tree delivery, Deacon's wariness seemed to ease up, too. She swore she even saw him cast a few purposeful glances toward the camera by the end of their day together. It was obvious the man was private, but Kate began to wonder if a little of that was for some other unknown reason and not so much due to shyness. He didn't seem nearly as guarded when it came to his interactions with his customers. From placing the tree topper on Blanche's tree to helping little Abbie Cornwall assemble the roof on her gingerbread house, it was clear Deacon had deep, meaningful relationships with the people he did business with.

Kate rose early the following morning. Breakfast in the main house was continental style with fat cinnamon rolls slathered in gooey, sweet icing, sliced orange wedges that reminded her of youth soccer snack times, and maple sausage links that made her mouth water. Deacon was right; freezer meals had fast become a distant memory. She figured by the end of her stay at Yuletide Farm, she'd not only gain experience as a tree farmer, but a handful of pounds, too. If she got to eat like this everyday, she wouldn't complain one bit about a little more padding around her middle. Every bite was well worth it.

After pouring coffee from the pot into her favorite thermos—the one with the Channel 14 News logo embossed onto the side—she made her way over to the onsite store to meet Marla for their morning of wreath making. As she stepped onto the porch, the air that whisked over her was crisp; invigorating like a splash of cold water.

She decided right then that if she could live anywhere other than the Sacramento Valley, it would be in the Sierras. The summers were mild and the winters often severe, but the mountain beauty was unmatched. And within the confines of a cozy cabin—or even barn loft—any weather condition could be enjoyed.

Today's conditions were unrivaled in wintery splendor. Soft clumps of white sprinkled tree branches, not yet melted even with the sun shining brightly in a cloud-less blue sky. Woodland critters scurried about, leaving little prints on the snowy earth and birds chirped in lighthearted chorus.

Nature was showing off and the thought of spending the day cooped up in a shop almost had Kate's smile slipping from her face. That was, until she opened the door to the farmstand store. If the month of December could take on visual form, this small space brought it to life to perfection. Thick garlands draped from the rafters, boughs of emerald green stretching wall to wall in impeccably spaced swags. There was a tree ornamented with rustic decorations. And the aroma. Kate couldn't get over the aroma. She pulled in a breath of the rich, sweet scent and filled her lungs to capacity.

"This one's my favorite," Marla acknowledged Kate's appreciation of the candle flickering on a nearby display table. "It's called An Heirloom Christmas. Isn't it heavenly?" Taking the candle into her hands, Marla strode over to Kate and waved it just beneath her nose. "Hints of clove and orange and vanilla."

"It's amazing."

"Haven't spent any time as a candle maker for *On the Job* yet?"

"Not yet," Kate said. "But I think I'll have to chat with my boss about adding that to our assignment list. I would love to learn how to make my own candles someday."

"Well, today you're going to learn how to make the wreaths we sell here on the farm. I've only got a handful left to assemble, but I sure could use your hand in making that happen."

"I'm ready. Do you mind if—?"

"If you get something on film first?" Marla anticipated Kate's request. "Of course not, dear. That *is* why I hired you, remember?"

It was a relief to hear Marla reiterate that. Kate's presence on the farm was mutually beneficial, even if Deacon didn't always make it seem so. Her show offered an unparalleled opportunity for publicity. She couldn't even keep count of the number of people who had contacted her over the years, boasting of increased sales and ventures as a result of appearing on her show. Things would be no different with the tree farm, Kate was sure of it.

She lifted her phone and set right in. "Good morning, Sacramento! Kate Carmichael here and today I'm with Marla Winters, the matriarch of the Yuletide Tree Farm. Yesterday, you got to ride along as we delivered our first round of rental trees, but today we're slowing things down to get a little crafty. Marla, would you mind showing our viewers just what we'll be up to?"

"I'd love to, Kate." Marla reached for one of the assembled wreaths and propped it in front of her. "For the last thirty years, we've operated a little farmstand on our property during the month of December. We sell ornaments, holiday decorations made by local vendors and artisans, along with some homemade edible goodies. But our bestsellers are always our fresh custom wreaths."

"And you make each one by hand?"

"We do. Every single one. My mother-in-law, Kay Winters, used to be the main wreath-maker, but after she passed, I took over the tradition and it's one I'm honored to continue."

Kate kept the camera rolling a few minutes more while Marla gave a brief tutorial demonstrating how to best adhere the Douglas fir trimmings to the frame to create a full, festive wreath. She showed off an assortment of embellishments from pine cones gathered on the property, to clusters of holly berries, to wire ribbons and made note of the sizes of wreaths available for sale, along with the prices of each.

Kate was impressed. Marla was detailed and thorough, but engaging in the way Kate knew her viewers would appreciate. It was easy to see why everyone sang Yuletide Farm's praises. Between Deacon and his mother, Kate was already doing the same.

"You're not half bad at wreath making, Kate," Marla teased when the women finally took a break to grab some lunch up at the house.

"That doesn't mean I'm half good, though." Kate laughed. She followed Marla into the kitchen and helped her grab the fixings for turkey sandwiches from the fridge. They placed the items on the tiled counter like an assembly line and got to work.

"Give yourself a little credit. You're still learning." Marla spread mustard across the face of a slice a bread and passed it off to Kate. "Let's make a few extras while we're at it. Deacon just texted and said he'll be stopping by for a quick bite."

At that bit of information, Kate's stomach did a full-on somersault. What had this man done to her that the thought of seeing him again made her react this way?

The front door creaking open and then thudding back into place made Kate's pulse uptick, but it was Deacon's expression when he came into the kitchen and their eyes locked that made her mouth go dry.

"Hi," he mouthed and she was about to do the same when a man Kate didn't recognize stepped around Deacon.

"Got room for one more at the table? I'm famished!"

"Joshua Evans!" Marla threw the mustard knife to the counter with a clatter and dove at the man for a hug. "You know there's always room for you at our table! I thought you were still in Santa Cruz. What brings you back up the hill?"

He swiped a knit beanie from his head and balled it up in his hands. His hair was an unruly mop of wavy bleached blond that fell clear to his shoulders and he had a tan few naturally sported during these winter months. He wasn't quite as big at Deacon, but was definitely tall with a lean, muscular build.

"I'm working at Sierra Slopes for the season. Teaching snowboarding lessons here and there and helping out wherever I'm needed around town on my days off."

"And today, that was on my truck, assisting with tree deliveries." Deacon came up next to Kate and took his place in the sandwich line. He gave her a warm smile. "How's wreath making going?"

"It's going." She handed him two slices of bread and a packet of deli meat.

"What Kate means to say is, *'It's going great.'* Her wreaths will be the first to sell out; I'm sure of it."

"Only because we'll need to deeply discount them."

Deacon knocked her with his shoulder. "I'm willing to bet people will pay top dollar to own an authentic Kate Carmichael wreath."

"Kate Carmichael?" Joshua hadn't even bothered with the actual sandwich and instead helped himself to a handful of turkey that he crammed into his mouth. "I knew you looked familiar!" He wiped his lips with the back of his hand and squinted his eyes as he placed her face with the memory. "You worked with my buddy, Chuck Cravens, a few summers back on a surfing piece for your show. I was there as an extra for one of the days you filmed."

"No way! Small world. That was so much fun. Chuck's a great guy and an excellent surf instructor. The fact that I didn't drown is a major miracle in my book."

"You been out in the water since?"

Kate shook her head. "I wish. Haven't really had any time."

"Well, if you ever find yourself in Santa Cruz during the summer months, look me up. I'd be happy to give you a little refresher. I'm sure Chuck would love to see you again, too. He talks about that television piece like he's reliving his glory days."

"I will definitely do that." Kate collected her constructed sandwich and plate and followed the hungry crew into the dining room to settle in. "How do you and Deacon know each other?"

"We go way back." Joshua had his mouth stuffed again. He was like a teenage boy with his ravenous hunger. The lack of manners fit the bill, too. "As in diapers, way back."

"These boys got into more trouble than two foxes in a henhouse back in their youth," Marla divulged as she scooted out her chair.

"Back in our youth?" Joshua feigned offense by clutching his chest and slumping back against his seat like he'd been dealt a fatal blow. "Are you implying we're old or something?"

"You're no spring chicken," Marla teased, her voice rich with laughter. "You two are getting up there, you know. I keep telling Deacon I'd like to get him married off sooner than later. I'd love to become a grandma while I still have the energy to be a fun one. But he has yet to honor my many requests to find a good woman and tie the knot."

"Can't say he didn't try with Jenny."

Like a fire alarm had been pulled, Deacon shot up from the table, his sandwich half-eaten on a plate he white-knuckled in his grip. "We gotta get going so we can finish up with the rest of today's deliveries."

"Ah, your customers are fine waiting—" Joshua began to protest.

Deacon yanked his buddy's plate out from under his nose. It wouldn't've surprised Kate at all if he hauled the man by his shirt collar into the kitchen, just to put a quick end to the conversation. In reality, all it took was one telling look and Joshua promptly retracted the foot he'd stuck in his mouth. "Yup. Gotta get on those deliv-

CHRISTMAS AT YULETIDE FARM | 95

eries. Thanks for lunch, Mrs. W. Nice seeing you again, Kate." He rose from the table and took a small, gentlemanly bow before following Deacon into the adjacent room.

Kate and Marla finished eating their sandwiches in a silence that felt stilted, but it was clear too much had already been said for one lunchtime. It wasn't for lack of questions on Kate's part, though. She had plenty of them when it came to Jenny. She recalled a similar reaction from Deacon when she'd commented on a rental tree bearing the same name, and again when she made a fleeting remark about the borrowed boots. It all seemed too coincidental not to be intertwined.

One thing was clear: whoever Jenny was and whatever she meant to Deacon, it was not up for any sort of discussion.

Something about that set off all of Kate's investigative bells. It was like an itch she couldn't scratch and despite her knack for digging around to discover the truth, Kate knew this was a story that would never be hers to expose.

DEACON

Deacon one-upped Santa by not only making a list, but checking it three times. Even with every item marked off, he still worried they had missed something. It was unlikely. Opening up the farm was an integral part of Deacon's Christmastime routine. Like the memorized lines of a holiday carol, he ran through his tasks without giving any purposeful thought to the parts that came next. It all flowed as naturally as a song.

Growing up, he'd heard stories of his mother cradling him in a swaddling blanket while she aided customers in the search for their perfect tree. His father and grandpa would work as a team to cut and bundle the winning selection before sending it off to its new home. Each year, Deacon would add to these memories. He was a toddler riding double atop his Dad's saddle while they made the rounds on their evergreen acreage. A young boy learning the mechanics of a handsaw and the strength required to cut through a sturdy trunk. A teenager trying to catch the eye of a beautiful girl, showing off his strength as he lifted cut trees onto car rooftops.

And now he was a man, trying to do right by all of the Winters men that came before him.

Deacon hadn't experienced a Christmas without the tree farm, and yet unjustified anxiety had a vise grip on his confidence. He still wasn't sure if he was doing the whole endeavor justice.

"Looks like we got ourselves a good little line forming in the parking lot." Cody stood next to his brother, eyeing the entrance from a distance. When he spoke, his breath left him in small clouds that hung in the chilly morning air. "You all set to open the gate?"

"As ready as I'll ever be."

Cody breathed into cupped hands for warmth and then rubbed his palms together vigorously. "You say that every year, and yet I'm still not convinced. This farm has been in your name for five years now, Deacon. When are you going to start acting like it actually belongs to you?"

"It's not mine. Maybe on paper, but that soil and those trees and this legacy—it doesn't belong to me."

"Of course it does because you're a part of it, Deacon. Just like your living rental trees, there's a living legacy here and you're smack dab in the very center of it."

Deacon gave his brother a sidelong glance. "Don't go getting nostalgic on me now. We've got trees to sell. I don't have time to get all mushy."

"I'll save the mushiness for a later date, then. Or I could just let Kate take care of that part."

"What's that supposed to mean?"

"I see the way you look at her, bro," Cody noted with an approving nudge of his chin. "I haven't seen you look at anyone that way since—"

"Don't say it."

"Fine, I won't. But I know when some girl's got your eye and Kate has more than that. Pretty sure she's got your heart, too." He jabbed a finger right into Deacon's chest.

"That's crazy. I hardly even know her."

"Sure. But you and I both know that doesn't really mean much. When you know, you know."

Taking a firm grasp on his brother's shoulders and twisting him in an about-face, Deacon gave Cody a little forward shove. "All I know is that our farm is about to open in less than five minutes and I don't think discussing my non-existent love life is the best use of our time right now."

"Roger that." Cody saluted and jogged toward the entrance, leaving Deacon to absorb their strange conversation. He didn't like that his growing attraction toward Kate had suddenly become public knowledge. Sure, his brother probably knew him better than anyone, but even Joshua had made a similar comment in the truck the day before. Something about a lovesick expression on Deacon's face when Kate came into the room. He wondered how his feelings could be so transparent. Maybe it was expected for a brother and a best friend to pick up on these things. He only hoped Kate wasn't as perceptive.

Who was he kidding? She was paid to be perceptive.

"What's the countdown?"

Deacon snapped from his thoughts only to see the very woman who had occupied them. She had on the same navy wool coat as the day before with a chunky knit scarf stuffed into the collar and bundled clear up to her chin like a turtleneck made of yarn. Her hands wore matching colorful gloves, making the set complete. Deacon figured she'd knitted them herself. He pictured her sitting cross-legged on a couch, bundles of yarn spread around her while she worked dexterously with the needles, hooking row by row together until she had enough to fashion into something wearable. Even though he'd conjured it up in his mind, it was such a heartwarming sight. But what surprised him the most was that when he envisioned her like this, she was in his living room and seated on his sofa.

How had his imagination transported her there?

"Deacon?"

He blinked, snapping the vision right out of his head. "Kate."

"Is it opening time yet?"

"Just about," he replied.

"You nervous?"

Deacon blew out a quick breath. "Is it that obvious?"

"Not at all." Her mouth bent into a reassuring smile. "Plus, what would you have to be nervous about? The farm is picture perfect."

"There's a lot of responsibility involved when creating a space for families to make memories. I don't take that lightly."

"You know"—Kate gave him a grin that teetered on the edge of a smirk—"You're a much more sentimental guy than I originally gave you credit."

"I suppose I'll take that as a compliment?"

"I hope you do, because I meant it to be one." She reached down and squeezed his hand, and even though hers was gloved, the skin on the back of Deacon's neck tightened at the gesture. "I'm only planning to do a couple interviews right after we open, so once that's finished up, I'm all yours."

"Oh really?" He couldn't help but perk up at her statement which was wrought with ambiguity.

"You know what I mean," she said but her tone held the flirtatious timbre he'd hoped to detect in it. More often than not, their recent conversations seemed to bear that same quality. He couldn't say he didn't like it. "See you in a few?"

"See you in a few."

In keeping with years past, the morning went off without a hitch. Like the opening of an amusement park, families squeezed through the entrance gates and then scurried off to their desired destinations. Some set straight out for the trees in hopes of getting first dibs on this year's selection. Others made their way to the farm-stand where Deacon's mother welcomed each guest passing through the doors with a hot cup of cocoa and a welcoming smile. Small children stopped at the holiday displays, squishing their chubby faces into the wooden cutouts while parents seized the photo-op, their phones lifted high as they called out posing instructions.

There was an expected air of cheer that warmed even the coldest of days and Deacon made a purposeful effort to soak it all in.

Even though he didn't intentionally mean to, throughout the morning his gaze repeatedly landed on Kate, seeking her out in every crowd, picking up her voice in every conversation. His attention fastened to her like a magnet. And he wasn't the only one to do that. People gravitated to her. Some recognized her from the show. When they did, they would begin by telling her which assignment had been their favorite. She would then share some little token of information that hadn't made it into the final cut; how she'd accidentally sheared the wrong dog as a pet groomer or had a fender bender as a taxi driver.

She knew how to make people feel special, like they were in on some little industry secret, but more importantly, she knew how to be real. She readily and openly admitted to her mistakes. There was humility there and Deacon realized this as the driving factor in her interactions. People felt comfortable around Kate because Kate was comfortable in her own skin—flaws, failures, and all.

It was the most refreshing, beautiful revelation.

As promised, Kate made quick work of her interviews and joined up with Deacon a little after noon. Things at Yuletide Tree Farm were in full swing with a steady stream of family-packed cars rotating in and out of the parking lot. Cody and a crew of high school boys worked tirelessly. Even though the farm allowed customers to cut their own trees, often a little assistance was necessary in that endeavor. They helped where needed and hauled trees up the hill before pushing them through the funnels that would bind the branches in a tube of red netting.

Watching his trees leave the property strapped on vehicle rooftops was always a joyful sight. Deacon knew before the day was over that these trees would be decorated with keepsake ornaments and serve as the Christmas centerpiece of the home. It was an honor to grow and provide something so meaningful to the season.

"Penny for your thoughts?" Kate cocked her head as though she could search out Deacon's reflective expression. They were monitoring things by the entrance, making sure there were still plenty of empty spots in the parking lot and redirecting traffic as needed.

"Just feeling grateful," Deacon said. "Grateful to have so many customers on our first day open. Grateful for such beautiful trees to sell." He gave her a thoughtful look. "Grateful for the nice company."

"I'm grateful, too. Grateful you don't have me out there hauling trees." She indicated in the direction of Cody with her gaze. "That has to be the twentieth trip I've seen him make with a massive tree balanced on his shoulders. How's he even going to be able to move tomorrow?"

"Oh, don't think you're getting out of tree hauling," Deacon challenged. "That's on tomorrow's agenda."

"Really?"

"Yes, really. You wanted the full experience, didn't you?"

"Absolutely. Nothing short of it."

"Then we can't leave out tree hauling," Deacon explained. "Don't worry. I don't expect you to lug a sixty-pound tree all by yourself. I'll be there to help. Plus, we've got lots of wagons and wheelbarrows on the property that we can use if we need to. It doesn't all have to be muscle and brawn."

"How come Cody's not taking advantage of those very helpful resources?"

"Because Cody will always do things the hard way if there's even a slight possibility it'll make him look good. He absolutely despises running, but joined the cross country team in high school all because some cute girl told him his mile time in P.E. was really impressive. Me, I'm less about making an impression and more about making things efficient."

"I, for one, think it's quite impressive how efficient your farm is, Deacon. Turns out you can have both."

"I appreciate that. I'd love to take the credit and say I'm the one who made it this way, but the truth of the matter is, I'm just the one keeping it this way."

"And you're doing a great job."

Deacon valued Kate's encouragement. She was a natural cheerleader and he hadn't realized how much he'd needed one in his corner, especially in recent years. "Did you get what you needed for your show?"

"I did. Lots of good footage that I plan to send to the station soon."

"Does that mean you're done for the rest of the day?" His voice lifted in hope.

"Only with one of my jobs," she said. "You know, I *am* working two these days."

"I'm pretty sure your boss will give you the rest of the afternoon off."

"You think so?" she asked, a brow bent up. "But it's opening day."

He gave the farm a quick once-over before his gaze circled back and landed on her. "Looks like things are under control here. They won't miss us for a couple of hours."

"Just what do you have in mind, Deacon Winters?"

"You're about to find out."

KATE

L eaving his tree operation on opening day seemed so out of character for the man sitting beside Kate. And yet there they were, loaded up in Deacon's truck, ambling down the back roads of his sprawling Sierra acreage. Majestic evergreens as tall as skyscrapers hemmed them in at every angle. Kate knew the Winters had a sizable amount of land, but so far she'd only explored just the small section of it near the barns and the main house. This portion lacked the symmetry and planning of the planted rows which, although undeniably beautiful, were almost commercial in feeling. Here, everything was natural, untouched, and uncharted. It was a winter wonderland.

"Almost there." Deacon glanced across the cab before he instructed, "Hold on."

Kate was about to reach up to grab onto the roof handle just as the vehicle dipped forward. The truck's shocks absorbed most of the impact as it jostled about on the slushy, uneven terrain. Kate had less luck countering her balance. She wobbled in her seat like a bowl of Jell-o.

"You good?" Deacon's hands gripped the steering wheel for control.

"I didn't know you offered rollercoaster rides on the farm." Kate braced herself with two palms on the dash when the truck suddenly lunged into a shallow embankment. The huge snow tires partnered with four-wheel drive to help the truck climb out of the snowy dip in the earth.

They rocked to a stop and there was a hiss from the truck when Deacon killed the engine. "We're here." He sat back in his seat. "You're not motion sick, are you?"

"I'm fine," Kate said, unwilling to admit that her stomach contents had been protesting the entire way. She was grateful their off-roading journey had come to an end because she couldn't promise she wouldn't become ill if the drive continued any longer.

"Normally I would take the horses or the snowmobiles, but with all the crowds up by the barns where they're stowed, I figured it would be easier just to take the truck."

Kate smiled, already feeling the wooziness dissipate.

"Ready?"

"Sure am," she replied, even though she didn't know what she needed to be ready for.

Deacon left the driver's seat and in keeping with his chivalry the night he took her to dinner, he came up to Kate's side of the vehicle to open her door and extended a hand. "I've got you."

She thought she had her footing, but as she stepped onto the running boards, her boot slipped from the slick surface and she fell straight into Deacon's arms. Her cheek slammed against his solid chest, making him stumble back from the impact.

"Whoa there." His hands moved to her arms to right her. "You okay?"

"I'm so sorry." Kate's mouth went dry when she looked up and saw the expression of concern cloaked on Deacon's handsome face. Their eyes locked.

"It's okay," he said, his voice quiet. Soft. "The boards tend to get icy."

Kate nodded so slowly she hardly felt her head moving. She hadn't released her gaze from Deacon's and each second their eyes remained locked caused her heart to beat faster, louder, almost to the point she could hear it thrumming like a drum line in her ears.

Deacon snapped from their trance first. "It's just a short walk from here." He all but jumped back, releasing her, but then something flashed across his eyes and he asked, "Mind if I hold your hand? Only because the land out here is a little challenging to navigate."

"Of course," Kate said. "I've proven to be kinda clumsy anyway, haven't I?"

"Not at all." Deacon was quick with his answer. "I just don't want you to fall in the snow and get all wet. It would make the ride back even more miserable."

Despite the nausea, Kate wouldn't categorize their drive as miserable at all. The opposite, in fact. "Thank you, Deacon. I appreciate that."

Walking through the snow, hand in hand with

Deacon, felt surprisingly natural. He guided her carefully, turning his head every once in a while to make sure she was following along without struggle. Luckily, the layer of snow on the ground was thin and didn't swallow their boots whole like Kate feared it might. Instead, it turned out to be an indisputably beautiful little hike, unlike any she'd ever taken and she had a small hunch the company had a bit to do with that.

After a brief trek, she could feel Deacon slow up his movements as his hand loosened its grip. "This is it."

Before them stood a tree, much like the others surrounding it. Kate had to crane her neck to take in its entirety, and even then, it required her to bend back a little to view the very peak branches. The evergreen loomed with grandeur, but Kate still wasn't quite certain what made this tree any different than the hundreds surrounding it.

"This is the first tree my great-great-grandfather ever planted on our farm." Deacon moved closer to the trunk. There was a small, engraved, gold plaque that he read aloud. "*Winters family tree. A million needles, a million more memories.*" He ran his thumb over the embossed lettering. "There was an entire forest of trees here when he settled the land, but this was the first tree he planted by hand and got to watch grow from a seedling. He even kept a journal that recorded its height year by year and when he couldn't measure it by hand anymore, he'd say, *'The family tree is as tall as a rail car this year,'* or *'It's as high as a bridge now.'* My great-great-grandmother loved this tree so much that they didn't even bother with an indoor Christmas tree. They'd just decorate this one out here each year instead. My grandparents did the same and so did my mom and dad. But my parents also liked having a tree in the house to pile presents under for me and Cody, so growing up we had one of those, too."

"Do you put up an inside tree now?"

"If I get around to it. Honestly, since it's just me, I don't always see the need for one," Deacon admitted. "But I brought you out here because this tree is what inspired me to start offering living trees for rent from our farm. I guess you could call this our original living Christmas tree." He shrugged. "I don't know, saying all of it out loud makes it feel a little silly. I just thought that it might be interesting to you."

"It's more than interesting, Deacon." Kate stepped forward. "It's inspiring. And beautiful."

He blew out a sigh. "I'm glad you think so. I think so, too. I love that even though the land was filled with trees, my great-great-grandfather thought to plant one just for himself. It was like he really knew he was creating a legacy. He was so intentional. I'm trying to learn from that and hope to be the same."

Kate wondered if he was intentionally trying to make her fall head over heels for him, too, because that was definitely happening. "Thank you for sharing this with me, Deacon."

"Sure. Happy to."

Shoving his hands into his coat pockets, Deacon shrugged his shoulders to his ears. "I suppose it was an awful long way to take you just to show you a tree that— for all intents and purposes—looks just like every other one out here."

"I've traveled much farther for a story before."

"You think this is for a news story?"

Kate's heart stuttered and her face flashed with a burst of heat, that awful, humiliating moment of saying the completely wrong thing. "I just…I mean, no. I get that not everything needs to be broadcast on television…"

"Do you think people would actually be interested to learn how my great-great-grandfather started this farm?"

Kate had assumed Deacon's first reaction was one of accusation but there was a lift to his voice now, a cadence of hope surrounding his question.

"I think people would *love* to hear about your great-great-grandfather, this tree, and his plan for the farm. This is really what it's all about."

The sweetest smile crossed over Deacon's lips. "I guess I don't really have a pulse on what people find interesting," he admitted, laughing at himself. "I was worried the whole drive here that you would think this was a complete waste of your afternoon."

"An afternoon spent with you wouldn't be a waste." Kate surprised even herself at how easily that confession slipped between her lips. "Thank you for bringing me. We don't have to do it now, but I'd love to film you and this tree before my assignment wraps up."

"It's a date," Deacon quipped and when Kate's eyebrow popped up, almost as a challenge to that statement, he amended, "Well, not like a date-date, of course. It's just a saying."

"Well, shoot. I was hoping it wasn't."

Deacon looked like someone had just heaved a sack of potatoes at him. He almost stumbled back. "What?"

"I said, I was hoping you meant it as a real date. Not just as the saying goes."

If Kate had told him she was actually one of Santa's elves on assignment from the North Pole, he couldn't have appeared more shocked. "You want to go on a date?" He paused as though she needed time to really gather her wits before answering. "With me?"

Insecurity began to unwind in Kate's belly. She pulled at the bulky knit scarf around her neck, almost willing it to swallow her whole. Things were rapidly growing awkward and she now feared that miserable truck ride back that Deacon had alluded to earlier. "I think maybe I've read things wrong."

"You haven't," Deacon said in a rush. "At least not on my end."

Their eyes met. "Oh."

"Kate, I'd love to take you out," he said. "I just wasn't sure if you'd want that."

"Really?"

"Yes, really." He shocked her even more when he stepped forward to take her hand in his. "How about tonight?"

Kate swallowed. "Yeah. Tonight's good."

"Great. Six o'clock?"

"Six is perfect."

They stood there for a beat, their eyes locked and hands joined, when Deacon suddenly swiveled around. "Ready to head back?"

She followed as they began their short hike to the

waiting truck, hand in hand, wearing matching smiles like teenagers who just found out their crushes were reciprocated. There was fluttering in her chest that Kate almost didn't recognize. Deacon consistently surprised her in the best ways and he took that up another notch when he slipped his hand out of hers and lowered his arm onto her shoulder to pull her closer into his side instead.

"You know, you're really beginning to grow on me, Kate Carmichael," he said, giving her a playful little jostle.

"Is that so?" She looked up at the man beside her, the one who, minute by minute, had effortlessly worked his way into her heart.

"It sure is."

DEACON

Deacon was nervous and he didn't often get that way.

In just a few short days, he had gone from being annoyed by Kate to being completely charmed by her. It was a surprising transition, to say the least. This pull to be with her was strong and it made him do things he wouldn't otherwise do.

Like leave the tree farm entirely in his brother's hands.

When Deacon returned that afternoon and asked Cody if he'd be willing to close up the farm that evening, Cody's eyes about tumbled from his head and his chin nearly hit the ground. He'd never been tasked with something like this, but not because he couldn't handle it. No, that was all due to the fact that Deacon would never dream of being anywhere but the farm the first day they were open to the public.

But Kate sure had him dreaming of other things.

Once Cody recovered from the initial shock, he assured his big brother that the farm was in more than capable hands. Marla was equally encouraging. Deacon noticed her telling smirk, though, like maybe she was in on something he wasn't. Right then, he wondered if there was more to hiring Kate than just the opportunity to drum up a little publicity for Yuletide. It wasn't the first time his mother had tried to play matchmaker. All of her previous attempts had backfired spectacularly but the verdict was still out on this one.

The afternoon sped by as things picked up at the tree farm. There was an expected wave of customers stopping by after quitting time and when five-thirty rolled around, Deacon checked in one last time with his brother before hurrying home to ready for his date.

Once there, he found himself staring at his closet. Each plaid shirt was less impressive than the one hanging next to it. He didn't have a clue how to dress for a date. All of his clothes were work-wear in both func-tionality and appearance. He did own one blue and green plaid button up that still had the tags on it, so he threw that on quickly and pulled a clean pair of dark denim jeans from his dresser.

His boots would be a problem, though. A quick shine didn't suddenly turn them into clean, presentable dress shoes, but it knocked the dirt off a bit and would have to do.

At a quarter to six, he gave himself a final once-over in the mirror, deciding at the last minute to leave his beloved cowboy hat at home and rake a comb through his overgrown hair instead. He felt naked without his signature hat. It had become his security blanket. But he wasn't sure it was fitting attire for their evening, and when he knocked on Kate's barn loft door just fifteen minutes later and she greeted him with an appreciative look that sent his heart racing, he knew he'd made the right decision.

"Wow." He felt her eyes travel from his head to his toes. "Deacon Winters, you sure clean up well."

"That's awfully generous."

"I mean it. I've never seen you without your hat. I was beginning to wonder if you had some big old bald spot you were trying to cover up."

He ruffled up his mop of hair with his hand. "Nope. In fact, I think I've got too much hair. I'm overdue for a cut."

"Nah." Kate shook her head. "I like it."

"Thank you. And you look beautiful." She had on a sweater in a deep plum hue that contrasted with her fair skin, and while she often wore heavy makeup for the camera, tonight she had used a lighter hand in applying it, revealing a smattering of freckles across the bridge of her nose. She was naturally attractive and Deacon knew if he didn't kick himself into gear, he'd be locked up right where he stood, fixated on this stunning woman in front of him.

"Thank you, Deacon." She reached behind the door to grab her wool coat from a hook in preparation for the cold that awaited them. When she went to slip her arms into the sleeves, she tangled in the bulky fabric.

Deacon moved closer. "Let me," he said as he took the jacket by the collar to allow Kate to shoulder into.

"Thanks. I appreciate the help," she said, then added, "You know, just a couple days ago you were pretty reluctant to offer it."

A vision of Kate sprawled on the barn floor with Sarge looming above had Deacon both chuckling and feeling a sick bout of remorse all at once. "I shouldn't have been so reluctant to help you and for that I'm sorry. I just—,"

She swatted his arm with the small clutch purse in her hands. "I'm just giving you a hard time, Deacon. All's well that ends well."

He sure hoped that was true.

Motioning for her to go first, Deacon trailed Kate down the creaky barn stairs and out to his awaiting truck. He had kept the motor running, hoping the cab stayed warm in his absence. Temperatures had dropped along with the sun and even for someone like Deacon who was used to this bitter cold, it was still uncomfortable. For Kate, it must've been downright freezing.

Once inside the toasty shelter of the vehicle, Deacon set out on the highway. He knew so little of Kate to know if she preferred a plan over a surprise, but he went with his gut and left their evening's events unspoken as he drove through the snowy Sierras. He figured if she really cared to know, she would ask. Kate wasn't timid. But the fact that she sat next to him contentedly quiet, her head angled out toward the passenger window, lips parted in awe at the breathtaking scenery, led him to believe she was fine with the unknown.

After a fifteen-minute drive filled with comfortable quiet, they arrived at their destination. The parking lot was nearly filled but Deacon managed to snag the last open spot. "Looks like they saved one for us."

Kate's eyes met his and then darted past him to the building at his back. "You brought me to church?"

"I did." He jingled his keys in his palm, his nerves rattling out with the noise. "I know it's not your typical first date setting, but tonight they're wrapping the gifts collected from last week's toy drive and I don't know,"— he shrugged—"I just thought something about that might be fun. But if you'd rather go to a movie or dinner, that works for me, too. Whatever you want."

"This is great, Deacon." She placed her hand over his trembling one. "I love it. Right up my alley."

"They'll feed us, too," he assured, knowing it was dinnertime and that she was probably just as hungry as he was. His stomach had growled at least three times during their drive. "And let me tell you, these church ladies sure know how to cook."

"Sounds like the perfect evening."

They hurried from the truck to the building, the low temperatures motivating them to move rapidly from Point A to Point B. But the church was predictably warm, both to Deacon's body and his spirit. He loved this little mountain town church. The wooden pews that were just the right level of uncomfortable to keep you awake during Pastor Tomlin's meandering but well-meaning sermons. The worn hymnals with loose spines and tattered pages. And the people. His friends, neighbors, and family that made up the congregation were treasures in and of themselves. This place was a haven to Deacon. Always had been. And tonight, he was so happy to share it with Kate.

"Deacon Winters!" They had barely crossed the threshold before Dottie Mason was racing to him with two flapping hands. "I told the gals you'd be coming by tonight, but they didn't believe me, what with it being opening day at the tree farm. I sure hope it was an enormous success. We've been praying, you know. Each week in our little prayer circle, we pray that this year will be even better than the last. We just love that you've kept the legacy going. Your father would be proud. Real proud." She rocked him back and forth in a hug that bordered on a dance move. "So wonderful to see you, son. Daryl's going to be thrilled to have some male company. He's outnumbered at the present moment."

When Deacon moved further into the room and Kate stepped out from behind him, Dottie's eyes when wide behind her wire rim glasses. "Hey, now. Who is this beautiful lady?" Without hesitation, she wrapped Kate in a hug and danced her into the church.

"This is Kate Carmichael," Deacon introduced. "Kate, this is Dottie. Dottie and her husband, Daryl, own the best feed store this side of the Sierras."

"We've got everything you'll need to care for all your animals, from hogs to frogs," she said in a singsong voice. "Maybe you've heard our little jingle on the radio?"

"Kate's not from here," Deacon answered for her. "She's based out of Sacramento."

"Oh, very nice. Very nice." Dottie's head swiveled around like an owl's at the sudden holler of her name.

She lifted a finger. "Sounds like I'm being summoned. You two make yourselves at home. We've got loads of toys to wrap and lots of papers to choose from. And if you leave hungry, well, that's all on you." She chuckled. "I think I counted something like thirteen casseroles in the kitchen. And the dessert table's looking pretty well-stocked, too."

"Thank you, Dottie. We'll get settled in."

"Nice meeting you," Kate added.

"You too, dear." Dottie gave a wink and then scurried off just as her name was called a second time.

Deacon took a breath. He looked over Kate in apology. "You overwhelmed yet?"

"Not even a little bit. I love how friendly and welcoming everyone is."

"Yeah? I was hoping you didn't feel ambushed. Dottie's sort of the unofficial greeter around here. She likes to know who's here and who's not and she'll sure as the day is long give you grief if you miss a Sunday sermon. Not much gets past that woman."

"Nothing wrong with a little accountability."

Deacon smiled, grateful she wasn't put off by Dottie's boisterous welcome. "Looks like the toy bins are just over there." He tipped his chin toward the far wall lined with round barrels that overflowed with donations big and small. "Want to pick out a few gifts and then find a place to get situated?"

"Sounds like a plan."

Moments later, they were seated at a long plastic folding table, a stack of presents ready for wrapping and several rolls of paper sprawled between them. Christmas carols filtered through the outdated speaker system. There was the white noise of chatter with bouts of laughter sprinkled here and there like sweet sugar. To Deacon, the room felt like an embrace—all of his favorite people, memories, and activities housed within these church walls.

It had been where he'd learned amazing grace, both in tune and in practice. When he'd lost his father back in his teenage years in an awful car accident just outside their farm, the church rallied around the Winters like they were their very own. Even though Deacon had grown up in the congregation, he'd pulled away in those adolescent years. He withdrew even more after his dad died. Any attempts to reach Deacon were met with opposition, obstinacy, and challenge. Eventually, as the years passed, there came a time when he needed that support again. Maturity and humility let him accept it this go around, and he was so grateful for these grace-filled people who welcomed him home with open, loving arms.

"Penny for your thoughts?" Kate glanced over at Deacon, noticing his pensive gaze.

"You owe me two cents now, you know," Deacon teased. "That's the second time you've asked me that."

"You should know by now I'm always happy to throw in my two cents." She kept her focus trained on the scissors and wrapping paper in her hands as she measured and cut a strip for her package.

"I see what you did there."

"Pretty great, right? I'm very punny." She made air quotes around the word and then reached across the table for the spool of clear tape. "But really, any chance you want to share what you were thinking? You seemed pretty lost in thought."

"Do you go to church?"

She ripped off a tab of the tape and played with the sticky side between her thumb and index finger. "I grew up going to one. My mom and dad weren't big on organized religion, but I had a childhood friend that would take me each week with their family. I loved it. There was this huge organ and when it was played, I could feel the music vibrate in my teeth. It was so loud. So powerful."

"I haven't heard you talk about your family before."

Kate placed the soccer ball she'd selected from the bin onto the strip of paper and held it there to keep it from rolling away. She looked at Deacon thoughtfully. "I'm an only child. To be honest, my parents didn't really even want any kids. The minute I graduated high school, they sold the house, bought two one-way tickets to Europe, and have been traveling in some form ever since. I think I was the only thing tying them to Sacramento and once that tether was cut, they were finally free."

"Do you hear from them often?"

"Depends on your definition of often. Every year or so they'll call to tell me to check in on my Aunt Sarah who lives in San Francisco, or they'll ask me to mail something for them. But I don't have a relationship with them, if that's what you're asking."

Deacon couldn't believe what he was hearing. That anyone would willingly choose to cut Kate out of their life was crazy. In fact, he already had an impossible time envisioning his life without her, and he'd only known her a few short days. She'd quickly woven herself into his routine, his thoughts, and if he were to be completely honest, he hoped into his future.

She'd offered a penny for his thoughts earlier, but he feared that revelation just might cost everything.

KATE

K ate wondered if she had possibly shared too
much. They'd continued chatting merrily as they
wrapped. Deacon had gotten them each a cup of
peppermint hot chocolate and when he returned, he
confided that he'd lost his father over a decade earlier
and how the church community united around him,
even after he'd repeatedly pushed them away. That part
didn't surprise her. For some reason, Deacon seemed to
have a difficult time letting people in. Letting people
help him. Letting them love him.

That last thought made her stiffen. She gulped down
a hearty swallow of the warm drink.

The truth was, Deacon really was lovable. Kate
could easily see it now. Not that she was falling in love
with the man. That was crazy. But she felt the slow soft-
ening of her heart and she knew if she were to spend
more than just her two weeks here, she'd find herself
never wanting to leave Deacon Winters behind.

"I don't carry any change, but a dollar for your thoughts?"

Kate laughed. "I was just thinking that I'm really enjoying my time here."

"Yeah, this is one of my favorite holiday events, too. Year after year, I'm still so amazed at the amount of toys our little town is able to collect for charity. It's heart-warming, to say the least."

"No. I mean, yes, this is great. I'm sorta terrible at wrapping but—"

Deacon suddenly erupted in a brief fit of laughter. "I'm glad you finally said it and not me. Those wrapping jobs are really something, Kate."

"It doesn't help that I picked weird-shaped items. A stuffed unicorn." She held up the offending toy and waggled it. "A ball. Race car. What was I thinking?"

"There's a reason all of the toys I selected came in boxes. I've learned a thing or two in my time volunteering here."

"What can I say? I'm always up for a challenge." Kate pushed the pathetically wrapped items aside and crossed her arms. "But what I was actually thinking was that I'm having such a nice time here…with you." She looked right into Deacon's hopeful eyes. "I don't normally get to spend much time with the people I'm on assignment with outside of filming. Definitely not doing charity work. Or sightseeing. Or going to dinner."

"Oh." The steadily growing smile slipped from his face in apparent disappointment. He cleared his throat softly. "I think I get where you're going with this. I can back off with—"

"No." The word flew from her mouth. "I want to spend more time with you, Deacon. That's actually what I'm trying to say."

Shock, then relief, lifted the corners of Deacon's mouth again. "You do?"

"I do." She pulled in a breath. "I'm just going to say it." She couldn't believe herself. She felt like a kid admitting a crush. Check yes or no and all of that. Gaining some courage, she pushed her hair back from her face with her palm and blurted, "I like you."

It was as if even time itself froze, shocked into stillness by her announcement. The Christmas songs switched from one to the other, but the pause between carols was drawn out and noticeable, unlike all the other smooth transitions. There was a muted lull about the room as if every other conversation had wrapped up right before her declaration. Even her heart felt like it hung on a beat.

It couldn't have been more than a few seconds but it felt like thousands, each passing one adding to her growing insecurity.

Deacon suddenly reached over and smothered her hand in his. "I'm glad to hear I'm not the only one. I like you, too, Kate."

Deck the Halls picked up, its cheery staccato notes like a rallying cue. Chairs scraped as people moved about the room. Laughter pulsed around them again. And Kate's heart continued beating in a familiar rhythm once more.

"You do?" she asked. "I was beginning to worry I might've overshared."

"Not at all. In fact, I'd love for you to share more. I want to get to know you, Kate. It's the whole reason I asked you to come here with me tonight."

"You know, I sort of thought maybe your mom was making you take me out. I mean, let's be real, I think it's pretty obvious she had some ulterior motives in hiring me."

"My mother has been trying to set me up for years now. I wouldn't put it past her," he admitted. "But no. I asked you here because *I* wanted you here." He glanced around the church at the now thinning crowd as volunteers wrapped up their packages along with their night. He directed his gaze back to Kate. "I know we're just about done here, but I'm not done with this." He waved his hand between them. "Are you up for one more surprise?"

DEACON'S HOME WAS EXACTLY HOW KATE HAD envisioned it. Minimal décor, but the few accents he did have strategically placed about the cottage were woodsy and masculine. A rack of magnificent deer antlers loomed large over a floor-to-ceiling stone fireplace. A leather reading chair angled out toward big picture windows that framed in the property and without even reclining in it, Kate knew it was the best seat in the house. There was a small galley kitchen and a dining table with just two chairs.

And there was a dog.

Deacon seemed like the type of man who would

own one. After all, he already had a few horses. Kate even saw a couple barn cats scurrying about the farm the other afternoon. Deacon appeared to be an animal lover. A dog fit into the mix perfectly.

But this dog was not man's best friend. Not Deacon's, at least.

"Rascal!" His gruff voice rumbled the minute the key turned over in the lock of the front door. "Dog! What have you done?"

Before she could even see the damage, the black Labrador had his tail tucked between his legs, slinking by them to retreat down the hall as though they might not notice the hundred-pound animal moving in their periphery.

"Rascal!"

When they rounded the corner, Rascal's guilt came into clear view. Sheets of gingerbread that had been resting on cooling racks were tossed about and crumbled with large, teeth-marked bites taken right out of the edges. Paw prints made of white icing marked the floor. Gumdrops and sprinkles and hard candies arrayed the kitchen like a sugary snowstorm had just blown through.

"That dog!" Deacon ground out through clenched teeth. He dragged a frustrated hand through his hair and then let out a massive sigh. "Well, this was the surprise."

"That you have a dog?" Kate teased, if only in a failed attempt to lighten the mood.

"I'm not sure why I thought Rascal could be trusted," Deacon scolded himself as he surveyed the disaster around them. "I knew I should've put him outside but it was just too cold tonight."

"I, for one, couldn't be trusted to be left alone with all that gingerbread goodness. It smells amazing in here, Deacon."

"You should've smelled them straight out of the oven. It was all I could do not to eat an entire wall before I picked you up. Maybe I should cut the dog a little slack."

Kate moved to the counter to begin wiping up Rascal's mess with a towel she found hooked on the refrigerator handle. "You made all of this? I'm really impressed, Deacon. Most people just buy the prepackaged kits."

"I just followed a recipe I found online."

"Still, that's more than I can do."

Deacon grabbed a broom stowed between the refrigerator and the wall and began sweeping up the candies. Round little balls rolled across the floor, skittering like marbles on the smooth surface. "I bet you could follow a recipe."

"You haven't seen me in the kitchen."

"That's not entirely true. I watched your pizzeria episode."

Kate felt heat collect on her cheeks. "I actually burned the first four pizzas I made before I finally created one that was halfway edible. The perks of good editing."

Deacon chuckled. "Gotcha. Well, what do you think? Should we scrap it all and try again?"

"I'm not one to ever turn down anything that involves this much candy. I say we go for it."

The two quickly tidied up Rascal's disaster, all while the dog looked on from his bed, his shame-filled eyes never meeting theirs in the way dog's inadvertently admitted to their guilt.

At a quarter to nine, they had a brand new set of gingerbread house materials, from freshly baked walls to icing in piping bags to little bowls of candies, sorted and ready for ornamentation.

Deacon had turned the radio on and a steady stream of holiday carols created a festive soundtrack for their night. His recently made fire sizzled and crackled in the hearth. Every aspect of Deacon's home embodied the terms warm and cozy, so the sudden flash of homesickness that swept through Kate's stomach took her by surprise. But it wasn't her home she longed for. No, the quick sensation that nearly had her wincing was the thought of leaving this place. Just this one evening shared with Deacon had her thinking that every future holiday spent in her lonely, sterile studio apartment would never quite measure up. For Kate, Christmas had always been a one-day thing, but here with Deacon, she felt the fullness of the season.

"Hold that side for me?" Deacon nudged his chin toward a slab of gingerbread between them. "I'm going to glue this wall on real quick."

He was great at construction. Their little cookie cottage went up quickly with Deacon as the foreman. Kate followed direction well, but when it was time to turn their house into a holiday masterpiece, she took the helm. Gumdrops became tiny shrubs that lined the walkway. Chocolate squares were now windows, piped white frosting the panes. Every piece of candy took on a new purpose until the little brown house was covered in so much sugary color that it could've been the residence of the Sugar Plum Fairy herself.

"I think we've run out of room," Deacon noted, squinting at their project as he searched for an empty spot for the round peppermint in his hand. "We've managed to cover every square inch of this thing."

Kate swiped the candy from his fingers and applied a dollop of icing to the back of it before pressing it to the front door. "Almost forgot the wreath."

"Good call." His hands hooked on the ledge of the dining table as he pushed his chair back to stand. "I'm going to get another cup of cocoa. Can I refill yours?"

"Yes, please." Kate passed off her mug. "I'd love that."

While Deacon busied himself in the kitchen with their drinks, Kate regarded him from her seat at the table. She'd been determined to peel back his many layers. It hadn't been as big a challenge as she had first thought. Deacon was guarded—that hadn't changed—but she could sense a slow and steady opening up and she knew if that trust continued to grow between them, there would be no telling just how close he'd let her get. She found herself wanting that more than anything. More than accolades from her boss. More than a pay raise or any sort of prestige at the station.

More than all of that, she wanted to get to know Deacon Winters. *Really* know him.

"Look what I found." Deacon returned with the hot chocolates, two mugs balanced carefully in one large hand. In the other, he held more gingerbread. "Almost forgot. Our finishing touches."

"Gingerbread men?" Kate took the mug and blew across the top of it, watching the steam dance in curling tendrils that snaked skyward.

"Yep. I made them earlier. They were just about the only thing Rascal didn't destroy." He lowered the cookies onto the table. "Care to decorate them with me?"

"I'd love to." Kate took a swallow of her drink before she picked up a piping bag and one of the cookies. "I'm going to make one of you. You make mine."

"Why do I feel like you're setting a trap for me?"

"Not a trap. Just a little fun."

Deacon snorted. "If you say so."

Kate found a jumbo marshmallow and smashed it on the top of the gingerbread man's head to make a version of a cowboy hat. She piped alternating colored lines for a plaid flannel shirt and used the rest of the blue frosting for his jeans. Licorice strips were cut into boots and chocolate dots became eyes. It certainly wasn't a dead ringer for Deacon, but it included all of his trademark looks and in truth, it wasn't a total failure.

"All done!" She proudly thrust the cookie into the air to show off her handiwork.

Deacon settled his yellow piping bag down and looked at Kate. "Me too."

"What do you think?" She held the gingerbread

man up closer for Deacon to inspect. "It's not perfect, but I think it kind of resembles you."

"I see what you did there with the cowboy hat," he said, nodding slowly. "And the boots. I like those. Nice work."

"What's going on here?" Kate waved her palm over the entire cookie in Deacon's.

"I accidentally broke your hand off when I was trying to make a little microphone for it." He held up the missing piece in question. "I tried to glue it back on, but it won't stay."

"I think we can fix that." Kate reached for both cookies, placed them onto the parchment in front of her, and layered a generous spread of icing on their feet. Then she planted them both in the front yard of their gingerbread creation, overlapping Kate's cookie character with Deacon's so her missing hand was covered up by his. "See? You don't even notice it now."

Something shot across Deacon's eyes. "Are our gingerbread cookies holding hands?"

"Well, mine doesn't really have one to hold, but yeah, I suppose they sort of are."

"Would that be okay?"

"I mean, sure. Why not?" Kate's brows pulled together as she studied Deacon's puzzled expression. "I don't think there are any rules when it comes to cookies holding hands."

"What about us? What are the rules there?" He hesitated with his words. "I guess what I'm trying to ask is, would it be okay with you if I were to hold your hand sometime?"

"Oh." She paused, surprised a little by the boldness in his question. "Yeah. Sure. I think it would be just fine," she finally answered with a confident smile. It almost shocked her just how okay that would be.

"Noted," was all Deacon said in reply before he stood from the table to begin cleaning up.

What Kate noted, however, was how her breath quickened at the thought of Deacon's large hand wrapped around hers. She could feel her cheeks pink and her palms begin to sweat. Deacon Winters was doing something to her alright, but where she felt it most was deep within her heart.

DEACON

It was just after ten. Not that Deacon had plans to sleep. He knew if he were to retire for the night now, he'd still spend several hours tossing and turning before his brain and body gave in to slumber. That was his usual routine and he assumed tonight would be no different.

But he'd noticed Kate's repetitive yawns, how they strung closer together as the night wore on. Sure, Deacon was still wide awake, but poor Kate appeared exhausted and her tired eyes all but begged to shut with each blink.

When they'd finished decorating their gingerbread house and everything had been put away, wiped down, and organized in the kitchen, he reluctantly suggested they call it a night.

"Can I walk you back?" Deacon asked when they were in the foyer. He held her coat open for Kate to slide into just like he had earlier in the evening.

"Absolutely. Please do." She began fitting the buttons on her jacket into their holes. "I know the barn loft is just a short walk down the hill from here, but knowing me, I'd get all turned around out there in the dark. Probably have to send out a search party and that's not something my coworkers at the station would ever let me live down. Believe it or not, but it wouldn't be the first time."

"You might be surprised how much the moon reflects off the snow. It actually lights up the whole forest. Come over here and look." Opening the front door, Deacon stepped onto the stoop. A brief evening storm had rolled through right after they'd returned from the church, leaving just enough snow in its wake to blanket the ground in a coating of puffy white. It had been beautiful to watch the flurries drift toward earth while they were tucked safely away in the warm comfort of Deacon's house. It was even more spectacular now to step out into the wintery aftermath.

"Wow." Kate's lips parted. "This is breathtaking."

"It is," Deacon agreed, but his eyes were fixed solidly on Kate and not the scene around them. Sure, he'd been with her all evening and while she always looked lovely, out here with the radiant moon highlighting the feminine slope of her cheekbones, its brilliance reflecting in her crystal blue eyes, he wasn't sure he'd ever witnessed such beauty in his life. It was enough to leave him speechless.

Kate turned her head and caught his spellbound gaze. "Everything okay?"

"You're beautiful."

Her mouthed twitched in the corner. "Oh."

"I'm sorry." Deacon shook his head, his brow buckling as he internally scolded himself for making things awkward. "That was really forward of me."

"No," Kate blurted. "Not at all. I'm just..." She blew out of a breath of mountain air that suspended in front of her lips. "I'm just not used to hearing that."

"That you're beautiful? Really? I find that a little hard to believe."

"No, not that. I've heard it before, sure. But it's usually from creepy old men or guys who just want to get on camera and think they can flirt their way in front of the lens." She shook her head, a momentary flash of disgust crossing over her face. "But I can't remember the last time I've heard it from someone like you. Someone I've actually *wanted* to hear it from. Someone who meant it as a real compliment."

"I'm sorry guys can be jerks." Deacon shoved his hands into his pockets as the two continued walking down the hill toward the barn. Fresh snow crunched under his boots, the only notable sound apart from their voices in the quiet of the December night.

"Women can be just as awful." Kate kept the pace at his side. "I'm sure you've had your share of crazies, looking like that and all."

Deacon pulled a face. "Looking like what?"

"You know, looking like you could be Mr. July in a cowboy calendar."

The stillness around them only magnified the rumble of laughter that shot from Deacon's mouth. If there had been any woodland critters nearby, he'd surely startled them all out of hibernation with that uproarious burst. "Okay. Gotta admit, I did not expect that."

"It's true, Deacon. You're quite a looker."

"Thank you?" he said, more as a question than an answer.

"You are most certainly welcome."

They continued toward the barn in relative silence, other than Deacon's low snickering that came and went each time he thought back on Kate's comment. He loved her no-nonsense ways. Her confidence. She didn't hold back both in her words or her emotions and he felt like maybe it was time to take a page from her playbook.

He slipped his hand from his jacket pocket and reached between them. When his fingers lightly grazed against her skin, Kate's hand stiffened initially, and Deacon's heart sped into a quicker beat as a shiver shot up his spine. Without giving it another thought, he wrapped his hand fully around hers and the light squeeze of her fingers against his assured Deacon that he'd read the moment correctly.

He'd made the monotonous walk from his cottage on the hill to the blue barn below countless times before. But during those treks he'd always wished for a shorter route. Tonight, he would've willed it to be a hundred miles long if he could. Holding Kate's hand while walking side by side in the freshly fallen snow was the perfect bow wrapping up their perfect evening. Even Rascal's little attempt at turning things on its head didn't take away from that. Nothing could ruin this, not even when Kate nearly lost her footing on a slick patch of ice and Deacon yanked her closer to keep her from slipping fully to the ground. Even that just resulted in them moving cautiously slower, taking their careful time and drawing out the walk even more. Kate pressed firmly against his side and slipped her arm through the crook of his elbow and suddenly everything felt completely right in Deacon's world.

Sarge and Bella greeted them first, little nickers of welcome calling out from their cozy horse stalls. As the couple made their way through the barn aisle toward the loft stairs, Milo, Deacon's calico barn cat, uncurled from a bale of straw and moseyed over, tail high in the air as he stretched his long body closer. As soon as he reached them, he began to loop between Kate's legs, brushing his furry cheek against her pants like he was marking his territory.

"Sorry." Deacon nudged the cat with the toe of his boot. "Milo's overly friendly. You can push him out of the way if he's bothering you. He doesn't really have any boundaries or know the meaning of personal space."

"Aww," Kate cooed. "Look at this cute little guy. He's not bothering me one bit." She released Deacon's hand and crouched down to pet the insistent feline. Deacon almost had to laugh at the silly envy that surged through his chest when he watched Kate fawn over the animal. What was happening to him that he would suddenly crave such attention from this woman? He hadn't felt this way since Jenny. That thought made him cringe, but it also filled him with strange hope. Hope that he really could find love again. Hope that heartache and heartbreak wouldn't always have a permanent residence within him.

Kate was here to provide Yuletide Tree Farm with a little holiday help, but Deacon sensed her helping him with things that had nothing to do with tree sales at all.

She was helping him learn to love again.

The second Kate's hand left Milo's fuzzy forehead, the cat's purring motor shut off. "Thank you for tonight, Deacon." She braced off her knees to stand back up and face him. "I had a really wonderful time with you."

"I did, too." He rubbed the back of his neck. "I mean, I had a good time with you, too. Not that I had a good time with me. That doesn't make any sense."

"I knew what you meant." She made a noise somewhere between a laugh and a sigh. "So, what's on the agenda for tomorrow?"

"Tree hauling and lots of it."

A glimmer of remembrance flickered through her eyes. "That's right! How could I forget? Then I guess I should probably head to bed soon so I'm well-rested for that task. Sounds like a big one."

"It is, but nothing you can't handle. You'll do great. And I'd offer to walk you up, but I'm honestly not sure those stairs can handle my weight," Deacon confessed, casting a look beyond Kate's shoulder toward the ailing loft stairs along the far wall. "I've made a note to take a look at them tomorrow. They seem to get creakier and creakier each day and I'm worried they'll completely give out sooner than later. I'd rather that not be tonight."

"I have noticed they're a little rickety. Thank you for checking that out. I know you have a lot on your schedule," Kate said, almost apologetically. "And you don't have to walk me up. We can say our goodbyes here." There was a palpable sense of expectation in Kate's gaze as she let out a soft breath. "Goodnight, Deacon."

"Night, Kate."

"Night," she repeated.

He felt the groove between his eyebrows form and prayed he didn't look as unsure as he felt. He clenched his hands inside his pockets and in one swift move, bent forward to press a quick kiss to Kate's cheek.

"See you at seven." Deacon spun on his heel, ready to hightail it out of there. He felt so foolish and unpracticed in the ways of dating and knew he'd blundered their entire evening with his silly nerves. Before he had gotten very far, Kate's hand caught his elbow and urged him to turn around.

"See you then," she said, pressing up onto her toes to leave a warm, slow kiss along his jaw. "And thank you again for tonight. It's one I'll never forget."

Those same words could've just as easily come from Deacon's lips. It was definitely a night for the books.

"Morning, Rascal."

The dog lifted his head from the bed and gave Deacon a look of sheer disbelief. Deacon had to give it to him. He wasn't sure he'd ever greeted Rascal with such exuberance. The poor dog probably thought his name was a curse word at this point. Deacon always did seem to say it in a certain disapproving tone. But there was ample reason for that and Rascal knew it.

Today, that hard edge to Deacon's voice was gone. Even when he nearly rolled his ankle on a piece of candy that hadn't gotten swept up the night before, he couldn't be mad at the dog. Nothing could ruin Deacon's high. He'd fallen asleep with a goofy grin on his face and woke up with the same smile plastered to it.

His date with Kate had been wonderful. They had shared playful banter but also delved deep to have real conversations about things that mattered. His heart broke when he'd learned that her parents weren't involved in her life. She didn't appear to let it bother her, but Deacon knew that had to be a strategically placed wall she kept up for protection. From what he knew of Kate, relationships were important to her. People were important to her. He doubted her parents were any different.

And by the end of the night, he felt like maybe he was becoming someone important to her, too.

Breakfast was a quick cereal bar and a thermos of weak, but hot, coffee. He gave Rascal a scoop of kibble and a scratch on his head before walking down to the storage barn to get the tree farm ready for opening. The sun crested high above the pines, sharp needles of light piercing through branches in star-like beams. This morning's walk was brisk and the cheerful pep in his step matched in rhythm with the Christmas tune whistled between his parted lips.

"Someone's in a good mood this morning," his mother noted the instant Deacon stepped into the big metal barn. She looked up from her task and gave her son a once over. "I take it your date with Kate went well?"

"Date with Kate," Cody snickered. He rolled past with a tree funnel in his arms. "That rhymes."

"Is it that obvious?" Deacon ignored his brother and focused his attention on his mother.

"Oh, you know, only for someone who has eyes," Marla teased, shrugging. "I don't think that grin could get any bigger, Deac."

"Or for someone who has ears," Cody shouted from outside the building. "Since when did you learn to whistle?"

"I've always been able to whistle," Deacon defended, not that it mattered. He knew his brother would find a way to razz him about all of this. It's just what brothers did. "But yes, my date with Kate was great."

"You sound like a children's book, bro."

"I'm so glad to hear it." Marla gave Deacon a sincere smile. "Kate is a wonderful woman and I'm happy you're taking the time to get to know her a little better while she's here."

Cody traipsed back into the barn, snow clinging to the tread of his shoes and a sheen of sweat developing on his face, the repetitive hauling of equipment an obvious exertion. Deacon almost felt bad that his brother was doing all the work while he and his mom stood idly by, chatting about his dating life. *Almost.*

He unscrewed the cap on his thermos and lifted the coffee drink to his mouth.

"And if things don't work out with her"—Cody huffed as he passed them once more with loaded arms

—"you've got a line of bachelorettes clamoring to go out with you."

Deacon gulped the mouthful of coffee and felt it burn his throat all the way down. "What's that supposed to mean?"

Marla and Cody swapped knowing looks.

"Seriously, what are you talking about, Cody?"

"You haven't seen?" Pulling her phone from her back pocket, Marla swiped the screen and then traded it for the thermos in her eldest son's hand. "Take a look at the comments on the Channel 14 News page. You've become quite the overnight internet sensation, Deacon."

He didn't know if it was the sting of the acidic coffee or this bizarre news, but his stomach soured. He looked down at the phone in his palm, his eyes roving over the comment section of the most recent post about their tree farm.

I wish Santa would leave that cowboy under my tree on Christmas morning! and *I'd get snowed in with that mountain man any day!*

Deacon's face flamed.

"What is this?" Like a hot potato, he tossed the phone back at his mother.

"Just a few harmless comments from desperate women." Marla returned her cell to her pocket and gave her son a little pat of encouragement on his shoulder. "Nothing malicious. You've made quite an impression with the ladies."

"*This* is your idea of publicity?"

"Deacon." Marla's expression quickly turned empathetic. "This just goes with the territory. I'm sure you've read some of the things people have written about Kate over the years. People tucked behind computer screens sometimes feel a little freer to say what's on their minds. Anytime you're in the public's eye—"

"But I didn't want to be in the public's eye!" He fought hard to harness the rising tone of his voice. "That's the whole thing, Mom. I just wanted to run our tree farm in peace and quiet again this season. No interviews. No cameras."

"Right, but my worry is that if we did that, it would be a *really* quiet year," she said. "As in totally silent. We need customers in order to keep our doors open, Deacon. If Kate's news piece can help funnel some more our way, then it'll be a success."

"But at what cost?"

"Oh, come on." She gave Deacon a little nudge. "Those comments aren't going to cost you more than a teeny, tiny bit of your pride. Honestly, I would think most men would be flattered to have some of these things written about them. You have quite a number of adoring fans."

Cody poked his head around the doorframe. "I even saw a marriage proposal in there. A gal named Stephanie from Auburn already has your colors and flowers picked out. All you'll need is the tux."

Deacon's eyes rolled so far it almost hurt. "This is ridiculous."

"Maybe." Marla shrugged. "But it's helpful. I took a long look at our numbers last night and yesterday's opening was the best we've had in years by far. There's no doubt in my mind that Kate's influence is the reason for that."

Deacon didn't like it, but if Kate's segment had been a total flop, he'd like that even less. If her success meant he had to deal with comments from a few silly internet fans, he'd make that sacrifice. His mom was right. He needed to push his pride aside and focus on what was best for the farm.

And that was selling trees.

At nine o'clock sharp, their gates opened to another crowd of eager families. People scattered this way and that, filling the farm with laughter, cheer, and memories in the making. Deacon seriously doubted this increase in patronage was all due to the extra advertising, but he couldn't think of another reason for it. He decided right then and there that he needed to quit his grumbling and finally become a team player.

The success of Yuletide Tree Farm depended on it and in the end, that was all that really mattered.

KATE

"One, two, three."

Kate grunted as she used every bit of her strength to lift her end of the Christmas tree onto her shoulder. She knew Cody bore the real brunt of the weight from the evergreen's thick log, but it would be a lie to say she wasn't still struggling a little. They'd moved so many trees. She'd lost count somewhere around the tenth one, but figured they were well into the thirties. Somehow, they all blurred together in one jumbled, pine needle-coated mess.

"You doing okay back there?" Cody called down the length of the tree.

"Yep!" Kate grunted again as she readjusted her side.

"We can set it down if you need a breather. This one is a mighty beast."

Each time she opened her mouth to speak, she used some of the energy she needed to hold on reserve in order to move this massive tree. She kept her words to a minimum. "I'm good."

The chatty little boy at her side, however, did not. "I asked him for a dinosaur but Dad said he can't fit one on his sleigh. But Sammy from school got a snowmobile last year. He fit *that* on his sleigh. That's huge!"

"Uh huh." Kate tried to stay engaged all while making sure she didn't dump the tree.

"So I wrote him *another* letter and told him that it didn't have to be a T-Rex or anything like that. There are plenty of dinosaurs that are smaller than snowmobiles, you know. I made a whole list and told him he could choose whatever one he wanted. I'm not that picky."

"Sure, you're not, Jackson." The boy's father caught Kate's eye and smiled. "I don't think poor Kate wants to hear all about your Christmas wish list."

"She doesn't?" Jackson looked offended on the worst level. He raced to catch up with his dad who kept stride near Cody's end of the tree. "But it has *dinosaurs*!"

"Roarrrr," Cody bellowed, stomping his feet with thundering motions. "Better watch out or this Douglas Fir-a-sauras just might get you. They've been known to gobble up little boys right around your age."

The child gave Cody the flattest look. "Yeah. That's not even a real dinosaur name."

"You certain about that?" Cody challenged. "I kinda feel like they're always changing them, aren't they? Discovering and digging up new ones all the time. You sure it's not some new dino breed?"

"I'm one-trillion, gazillion percent positive."

"Got it." Cody let it be while they lugged the tree the rest of the way. When they reached the storage barn, Kate let her side drop to the ground before Cody was ready with his, which made him stumble backward with the unexpected shift in weight "Whoa, Kate. Gotta let me know next time before you let go like that."

"I'm sorry." She heaved out the breath she hadn't realized she'd been holding the entire way up the hill. "Those trees are heavier than they look. And I think they get heavier each time."

Cody snickered. "Why don't you run into the store and grab some hot chocolates for Jackson and his dad here. I'll shoot this tree through the funneler to get it all bundled up and ready to load. Then we should think about taking our lunches. We're long overdue for a break."

Kate didn't love the idea of leaving Cody high and dry to finish up with this sale, but her muscles protested so loudly she could hardly think of anything else. A short break would be more than welcome.

But before she took Cody up on the offer, she stepped closer to Jackson, bending down to meet his eye. "Have you thought of asking Santa for dinosaur eggs instead of a real dinosaur?"

"Dinosaur eggs?" Jackson's big green eyes turned to saucers. "No. I didn't think of that."

"He can fit lots of those on his sleigh. Then you'll be able to raise them right from the beginning. I've heard if you raise a dinosaur from the time it's an itty, bitty baby, it'll be bonded to you for life."

"Then I wouldn't have to worry about it eating me!"

A dawning of understanding clicked across Jackson's face. "I was really worried about that, you know. I don't want to be eaten by a dinosaur. How many eggs do you think Santa Claus can fit?"

"Oh, lots, I bet." Kate straightened back up. "Now I'm going to go grab those hot chocolates Cody promised."

"Daddy? Can I go with Kate?" Without reservation, Jackson reached up to grab ahold of Kate's hand.

"The hot cocoa is just in that little shop." Kate pointed in the direction of Marla's farm store. "We won't be long."

"As I recall, there are lots of breakables in there, Jack. Why don't I join you two just to keep an eye on you and make sure nothing gets knocked over?"

"I'm not going to break anything, Daddy." Jackson's little grip tightened around Kate's hand. "That was only the one time."

"Jackson hasn't really comprehended the whole 'look with your eyes only' thing yet." The boy's father moved closer to Kate. "He's a sucker for shiny things."

"A hard concept to understand when you're only... seven?" she guessed.

"Seven *and a half*," Jackson corrected. "How old are you?"

"Jackson," his father scolded. "It's rude to ask an adult their age."

"Why?"

"Well, because—"

"I'm twenty-eight," Kate answered. "And three-quarters."

"That's old," Jackson said without missing a beat. His father's face instantly paled.

"Not as old as a dinosaur, at least." Kate shrugged. She bumped the door to the shop with her hip and then held it open for Jackson and his father to pass through. "Come on in. Let's get ourselves some of Marla Winters' famous hot chocolate. I hear it's even better than the stuff Santa's elves drink."

There was a lull in the store, all of the crowds enjoying the crisp wintery weather outdoors at the moment. Marla stood behind the counter and when she pushed the register drawer closed, she looked up and caught sight of the chatty trio. "Did I hear someone say they had a hankering for some hot chocolate?"

"No. We just want to drink some." Jackson lifted his hand to touch a bright red, glass ball ornament on a nearby tree and as quickly as he made the movement, his father was right there to halt him.

"Why don't you hold onto my hand, too, Jack." He snatched up his son's free hand. "That way we can be sure nothing gets broken."

"How am I going to drink my hot chocolate then?"

"We'll save that for when we go back outside," Kate suggested.

Jackson scrunched up his face in a disappointed grimace. "Alright," he sighed. Then, as quickly as his frown appeared, it flipped up into a smile. "Do you sell *dinosaur* eggs here?" he asked Marla.

"Hmmm." She thumbed her chin. "No dinosaur eggs, but I believe Santa can get his hands on those. I hear he's got some really rare Hot Choc-a-saurus Rex ones that can only be found in the North Pole."

"You guys sure like to make up dinosaur names around here," Jackson said with a squeak in his voice. In unison, the adults pealed with laughter. "What? You do."

"Jackson does know his prehistoric animals, I'll give him that," his father noted. "Hey buddy, should we look around for something for Grandma Tori while we're here? I think she'd like one of those good smelling candles over there on that table. Want to help me pick one out?"

"I'll grab those hot cocoas while you do that." Kate let go of Jackson and moved toward the counter. "How's the morning starting off?"

Marla waggled her shoulders. "Can't complain. The shop's a little slow, but Deacon texted and said overall attendance is through the roof. I think everyone's outside enjoying this gorgeous weather while they can. A big storm is supposed to blow through tonight."

At the mention of Deacon's name, Kate felt the hairs rise on the back of her neck. "Has he been by the store yet? I haven't seen him around much today."

Their plan had been to cut and haul trees together, but Deacon moved Cody over to that job when the teenage boys that helped out during the season needed some extra assistance with crowd control in the parking lot. She hadn't realized it would be an all morning sort of thing.

"He actually said he's on his way over soon for lunch." A glint in Marla's eye acknowledged Kate's question. "If you stick around a few minutes, I'm sure you'll catch him."

"Oh, I…" Kate fumbled with her words. "I don't need him for anything…I was just wondering what he was up to."

"I'm sure he'd like to see you, too." Marla grinned and followed Kate's gaze that landed on the father and son duo at the opposite end of the store. "You're really good with kids, Kate. When the three of you walked through those doors, hand in hand, well, you almost looked like a little family. It was a very sweet sight."

That thought shot through Kate's stomach. "We did?"

"I had to do a double-take."

"Jackson is a super friendly little guy. I think he takes to anyone who will listen."

"But not everyone listens to children. Many people outright ignore them. You have a way with kids, Kate. It shows."

Hearing that compliment made her heart squeeze. She did love children but didn't often have the opportunity to be around them. "You think so? I don't have a lot of experience with kids, really. No nieces or nephews to spoil and love on. But I hope to have a whole crew of my own someday. Four or five kiddos, at least. Just haven't found the right man who shares that hope for a big family. Or the right man in general."

Marla's lips curled into a smile. "I wouldn't think you'd have any trouble in the dating department, sweetie."

"You'd be surprised. Honestly, sometimes it's a little

hard to know if someone is really interested in me or just in what I do for a living. When it comes down to it, I'm just a local news personality. But it seems like some guys still want their little shot at fame, even if it's just on local T.V. Sometimes it's really hard to know a person's motive."

"I can understand that. The truth is, you can never fully know someone's true motive. You just have to trust that good people are out there and that when the timing is right, they'll show up in your life."

The chiming bell above the door pulled Kate right out of the conversation. Her eyes landed squarely upon Deacon who took up the entire frame in his Sherpa-lined denim jacket buttoned up near his neck and khaki work pants paired with leather boots to round out his attire. And of course, he had his signature white cowboy hat perched atop his head.

He looked as handsome as she'd ever seen him.

"Speak of the devil," Marla said through and all-knowing smirk. She clapped a palm to the counter and pushed off. "I'm going to go fetch those cocoas for you all. Be back in a jiffy."

"Kate." Deacon locked eyes while he moved across the store to come up by her side. "How have things been going with the trees? I'm sorry I had to leave you in such a rush with Cody like that. There was a fender bender in the lot this morning and I can't say it wasn't our parking attendant's fault. I figured I should stick around there for a while just to make sure nothing else like that happened."

"Everyone's okay?"

"Oh, yeah. Thankfully. Just some scratched paint that'll be easy to fix."

"Glad to hear it," Kate said. "And things with Cody have been great, actually. But those trees are sure a lot heavier than they look. My shoulders have never needed a massage more than they do right now."

"I think I might be able to arrange for that." The quick, flirtatious remark had Kate practically gasping. Not that the thought of Deacon's large hands on her shoulders was an unwelcome one. He flipped the subject before she had a chance to become fully flustered. "You eaten lunch yet?"

"Not yet. I was just in here grabbing some hot chocolate for Jackson and his dad—"

"I think we've found the perfect holiday candle for Grandma." The man and his son stepped up to the cash register with a small, glass jar in hand. "What do you think, Kate?" He unscrewed the cap and waved the candle under her nose. A rich aroma of cinnamon, clove, and sugar emanated from the wax. "Is this the one?"

"That smells like a Christmas kitchen in a jar. The perfect choice," she agreed.

The man looked around the room almost expectantly. "I thought there was a lady here earlier that might be able to check us out."

Deacon scooted around the counter. "I can ring you up. Mom's gone to grab some hot chocolates." He reached out for the item and then punched a few buttons on the register. "That'll be ten thirty-seven."

Jackson's dad fished through his wallet, tossed a few

bills onto the wooden tabletop, and directed his attention back to Kate while Deacon counted out his change. "So, Kate, I hope this isn't too forward, but Jackson and I both had a really nice morning with you. We were wondering if you might want to hang out with us again sometime. Maybe come over and help us decorate our new tree?"

"Oh." Kate's mouth fell open, entirely surprised by the invitation. "I, um…" She could feel the heat of Deacon's eyes upon her as he quietly watched the exchange from the other side of the counter. "I had a really nice morning, too."

"My daddy's asking you out on a date, Kate," Jackson said bluntly. "So, will you go out with him or what?"

Jackson's father seemed like a decent man, but Kate didn't even know his name, much less anything about him. She was used to proposals like this and often had a polite rejection at the ready. But the truth was, in any other scenario, she probably would've taken the man up on his invitation. He was everything she often looked for in a guy: caring, good with kids, respectful and even noticeably handsome.

But her heart wasn't on the market at the moment. It didn't feel like it was, at least.

"I'm sorry," she said, after a pause that made the situation even more strained. "I'm currently seeing someone."

A flush of embarrassment reddened the man's cheeks. "Oh gosh. My apologies. I figured that would probably be the case, but I would've been kicking myself the entire drive home if I didn't ask. I've learned that sometimes you have to just put yourself out there. Seize the day and all. No regrets."

Deacon slipped the candle into a paper bag stamped with the farm's logo and slid it across the table top, still silently eyeing the conversation playing out before him.

"I completely understand," Kate assured. "And I'm very flattered. I had a great morning with both of you. And Jackson? If you successfully hatch any dinosaurs, will you think about naming one Kate-a-saurus?"

"That's not a real name either." He slapped his forehead with his palm. "You guys need to read a dinosaur book or something." The little boy rolled his eyes with dramatic flair. "Finally! There's our hot chocolate!"

"Sorry about the wait." Marla scooted up to the group with three Styrofoam cups of cocoa strategically gripped between her fingers like a triangle. She lowered them steadily to the counter, taking great care to make sure no hot liquid sloshed over the top. "Had to make a new batch, but I promise this one is extra chocolaty."

"What do you say, Jackson?"

The child looked up at Marla. "About time!"

"Jackson!" his father hissed. "That is extremely rude. That's not how we talk to adults."

"Sor-*ry*. Thank you for the hot chocolate," Jackson tried again in a flat voice.

"Hey, no apologies necessary. I don't like to wait for my hot cocoa either," Marla said with a grin.

After a brief goodbye that ended with Jackson rushing back into the store to give Kate a final hug, the space fell silent, save for the chugging sound of the electric toy train that circled the display tree.

"I'm going to head outside to check on Cody real quick," Marla said, though Kate knew full well that Cody didn't need checking on. "Be back in a few."

It wasn't until the door slipped shut behind his mother and the trill of the bell above it quieted that Deacon broke the silence.

"You're currently seeing someone?" His strong brow buckled over his eyes that bore just enough intensity to make Kate wary. "Or is that just a line that you use to keep guys from hitting on you?"

"I am seeing someone." She looked right at him. "I see you right now."

He laughed a little but it was tight and cautious. "I can't tell if you're being serious or if you're just joking around."

"I'm being serious."

Deacon stepped around the counter. "Is this what we're doing here?" He came up close to Kate, so close she could smell his pine-scented cologne and feel the warmth of his large body as he hovered over her. "Seeing each other?"

"I mean, I'd like for it to be. But I totally understand if that's not what you want—"

Her words were cut off by his huge arms wrapped around her. The move was so fast, so unexpected, but the act so soft and sincere that Kate nearly melted right where she stood. She had to purposefully lock her knees so they didn't completely give out beneath her. Deacon was a force, no question, but he held her like she was a precious gift. Like he was afraid she might slip through his arms if he didn't gather her up and keep her safely there.

If she hadn't already fallen for the man, this would've totally sealed the deal.

"Cody's fine," Marla's cheery voice served as a shockwave that propelled the couple out from each other's embrace. "Oh!" She all but skidded to a halt at the store's entrance. "I'm sorry. I didn't mean to interrupt—"

"You're not interrupting anything." Deacon continued his backward steps. His boot caught on a table leg and the items on it clattered like China in a cabinet during an earthquake. He righted a ceramic reindeer figurine just before it had the chance to teeter completely over. "Everything's good here."

"I can see that." Marla's intonation lifted. "I'll just leave you two—"

"I've actually got to get back to the lot to check on the guys." Deacon paused. He spun around and aimed his gaze at Kate. "Any chance I'll *see* you later?"

"Yes." Kate beamed. "You absolutely will."

DEACON

"Stay safe out there." Deacon drummed against the sedan's roof with his palms. "It's really starting to come down. I just heard the forecast for tonight is calling for at least eight inches of snow."

"Thankfully, we're only a couple miles down the road. Should be okay." The driver poked his head out the window and flicked his fingers on his forehead like a salute. "Thanks again for always growing such beautiful trees for us to enjoy. We can't wait to get this one home and all set up."

"It's our pleasure. Merry Christmas to you all."

"Same to you."

The sweet, little family of four drove off the property and Deacon followed behind to lock the gate as their taillights disappeared in the steadily drifting snowflakes. It had been a full day with more customers than they'd ever had in a single shift, if Deacon's mental tally served him correctly. He was dog tired, but he kept repeating the mantra to himself he'd get a break after the new year. This was just the final push.

The thought that used to provide such relief now evoked a different sensation within him. Come Christmas, Kate's news piece would be wrapped up and she would move on to her next assignment. There would be no reason for her to stick around Yuletide Farm. Deacon wasn't so foolish as to think a budding new relationship would be enough to tether her here. A future with Kate had a time limit and he wondered if those few weeks would be worth the heartbreak that would inevitably follow.

He wasn't sure he could survive another one.

As the snowfall picked up, white flurries cascading through the bitter cold sky, so did Deacon's steps. The promise of a hearty meal spurred his legs into another gear, and when he finally made it to the main house, that fulfilled hope warmed him more than the fire that blazed inside the pellet stove.

"Just in time, Deac," his mother called out from the kitchen upon hearing his entry. "Care to come in and help me cut up this roast?"

"More than happy to." Deacon rounded the corner, not at all surprised by the sight that greeted him. It was much like the one he saw the day before when he and Joshua stopped in for lunch to discover his mother and Kate already preparing a load of sandwiches for the group. Tonight, Kate had a cranberry red apron tied around her slim waist, flour dusted on her pert nose, and her hands wrist-deep in a lump of dough.

"Kate's making dessert for us."

"Let me guess," Deacon pondered. "You spent some time in a pie shop once?"

"Bingo. But as with all of my culinary endeavors, I can't promise this will taste any good. Or even be edible, for that matter."

"If you made it, dear"—Marla pressed her shoulder to Kate's before she skirted around her in the small kitchen—"it'll be just perfect. Now Deacon, get to carving that roast. I'm going to head to the barn to feed the horses their dinner and when I come back, I'm hoping we can all sit down around the table and do the same. I'm famished."

"Sure thing, Mom. I'm on it."

Marla gathered her coat from the hook next to the back door and bundled herself against the storm that picked up outside. "I'll be back in ten," she said and Deacon couldn't help but notice the mischievous glint in her eye. "I'll knock this time before I barge in."

"Not necessary, Mom. I'll just be cutting the roast."

"And I'll be finishing up these pies," Kate added as an alibi.

"Sure. Okay." Marla winked, cast a nonchalant look above their heads toward the pitch of the ceiling, and pulled the door tightly shut behind her.

As he lifted his head, Deacon had to keep from audibly groaning at his mother's audacity.

"Has that always been there?" Kate aimed her gaze toward the sprig of mistletoe hanging from the rustic beam directly above them.

"No. Definitely not." Deacon reached up to pull the greenery free.

"You don't have to do that." Kate's fingers busily crimped the edges of the pie so she didn't look at him when she said it, but she nudged her chin, indicating to leave it be. "It's sort of festive. I say leave it up."

"Really?"

"Yeah?" She shrugged, still focused on the decorative rim of the pies. "Why not?"

"Well, for one, you might get caught under it with Cody. He does live here and the guy spends a ton of time in the kitchen rummaging through that fridge. You don't want to fall into that trap."

"Oh, Cody's not so bad."

"Not so bad?" Deacon said through a chuckle while reaching into the cutlery drawer to locate the carving knife. He found the one that belonged to his father, the very knife he'd used each Thanksgiving to carve the turkey and every Christmas to slice the prime rib and Deacon felt a pang of sadness at the long-lost memories. He shrugged off the mounting sadness and said, "I beg to differ, but that's just my opinion. I'm sorry I abandoned you like that, but I didn't feel comfortable leaving the boys to man the lot after what had happened with the fender bender earlier in the day. Did you at least have an okay time with him?"

"We had a great time. Honestly, Deacon, I've loved every minute of my time here so far."

"Yeah, I feel like maybe you've already forgotten our first interaction."

"I haven't forgotten it, but I understand it now. This place is unique, Deacon. Your family has created something really special here and I get how protective you are over it. I'm an outsider. You were right to be wary of me at first."

Deacon lifted his eyes from his work. "I'm cautious by nature. Can't help it, really. But I've been working on it. It's something I'd like to change."

"I don't necessarily think it's a bad thing." Kate took a few steps across the kitchen and bent down to pull open the oven door. She placed two expertly assembled pie crusts onto the racks. "It's okay to guard what's important to you."

Lifting a stack of sliced meat onto the platter his mother had set out for him, Deacon paused. "I felt that way today. Like I wanted to guard something important to me."

"Yeah?" She shut the oven door and turned around, pressing her backside against the counter as she gave Deacon a puzzled look. "How so?"

"I don't know. Maybe it's silly, but when that guy asked you out, I felt something I haven't in a long while."

"Jealousy?" A single eyebrow winged up in curiosity.

"No, not that. I don't think it was jealousy, at least." Deacon rested the carving knife on the tiled counter, his expression pensive. "I actually felt really grateful when you told him you were already seeing someone. It was such a relief to learn that my feelings for you weren't one-sided."

"They're not one-sided at all." Kate's bright eyes held his for several measures before she snapped from her reverie, her hands twisting anxiously in the apron tied around her middle. "This is a first for me. I've never fallen for someone on the job before."

Deacon prayed it wasn't visible, but he startled at the words. He'd been so wrapped up in whatever was growing between them that he'd nearly forgotten Kate's real purpose here on the farm. She did her work so effortlessly—conducted her interviews so seamlessly—that he often didn't even notice her camera rolling. But when it all boiled down, this was first and foremost a job for her.

"Maybe I shouldn't've said that," she backpedaled.

"No." He moved closer. "I feel the same. I wasn't expecting you."

Kate nodded. "Right. Your mother probably should've been more honest about hiring me—"

"No. I mean I wasn't expecting *you*." He motioned between them. "Or this. Any of it."

He could feel the mistletoe hanging above them like a guiding push, its weighty presence nudging him closer.

Kate sensed it, too. Her throat pulled tight with a swallow and her eyes looked everywhere but at the taunting little bundle of green dangling overhead. "I wasn't expecting any of this either."

She took the step that brought them within inches of one another.

"Is it okay if I…?" Deacon gulped. "If I…?"

Kate's shoulders rose and fell and just when she parted her lips to finish his sentence that suspended unanswered between them, a blast of mountain air whirled into the kitchen, engulfing the room in a teeth-chattering chill. The back door flew open so forcefully it nearly dented the drywall on the opposite side, crashing loudly on its hinges.

"Mom!" Deacon shouted at the sight of Cody angling through the doorway with Marla in his arms, struggling and out of breath like he'd just run a mile. "What happened?"

Deacon hauled his mother from his brother's grasp and together they rushed into the family room to settle her onto the couch directly in front of the pellet stove.

"Mom, are you okay?"

Marla's face retained the pallor of a ghost, but her tone remained spirited. "Oh, I just slipped and fell. Nothing to write home about."

"Her ankle's already swelling quite a bit," Cody noted over Deacon's shoulder. He scrubbed a hand down his face and paced back and forth along the wool rug. "I think there's a decent chance it's broken."

"It's not broken," Marla snapped. "I've just got weak ankles. Always have."

"We need to get this checked out, Mom." Deacon slid his mother's boot from her foot and lowered the shoe to the floor, then lifted her leg a touch to examine the injury. "Cody, do you think you would be able to go out front and get my truck warmed up for us? I'll bring her out after she gets some pink back in her cheeks. You're looking awfully pale, Mom."

"Sure thing, bro."

Marla's hand flew up. "That won't be necessary, boys. I'm not going anywhere. I'm telling you, it's not broken. I just rolled it on that dang loft staircase. It's just a sprain. It'll be good as new in no time."

A hiss slipped between Deacon's lips. "I knew I should've fixed that already."

"Well, now it *really* needs fixing because it's currently missing two rungs." Marla looked up at Kate who stood behind the two concerned men and locked eyes. "I remembered you asked about getting a few extra towels and I was just leaving them up there for you, dear. Or trying to, at least. I didn't make it all that far before I came crashing down like Santa tumbling down a chimney." She laughed at her own comment and then waved at her sons. "Now, help your mother up so we can get to eating that meal that smells so delicious."

"Nope. You're not going anywhere," Deacon said with conviction. He nudged his mother's shoulders back toward the couch cushions when she tried to bolt up from the sofa.

"But I'm hungry."

"I'll grab the T.V. tray," Cody said to his older brother like he could read his mind. Deacon nodded, liking the idea.

"And I'll fix you up a plate." Kate didn't wait for a reply before quickly disappearing into the kitchen.

Left alone with his mother, Deacon lowered to kneel next to her, just like he used to when they would say his nightly prayers at his bedside as a boy. "Mom." Though still insistent, his voice was now coated with concern. "I know you don't want to, but you've got to let me take you in to get this checked out."

Marla's lips buttoned in defiance and she shook her head in tight, narrow motions. "You know I can't do hospitals, Deac. Not since everything with your dad…"

Deacon knew that. He'd hated them, too. The cold, sterile rooms that reeked of disinfectant. The clinical news from doctors lacking bedside manners. Of course, he knew not all hospital experiences were like that, but they'd had a terrible, life-altering one and the thought of being back in that building was enough to sour Deacon's stomach.

But his mother's health was still the main concern here.

She cupped her hands around his, compassion filling her motherly gaze. "I'm *fine*, Deacon. Honestly. It's just a sprain. I've had many of them over the years. You know that. Just a couple days' rest and I'll be good as gold. Trust me on this, okay?"

He relented with a sigh. There was no telling this woman what to do, of that he was well aware. "Then at least let me get you something for the swelling. I really don't like the way it looks. Do you happen to know if there's any ice in the freezer?"

"If not, there's an entire farm-full just outside."

Deacon chuckled. "I supposed there is, and more coming down as we speak. I'll go fill a plastic baggy with some snow and then help you get settled in and situated for the evening. Cody's up in the attic looking for that old T.V. tray and Kate should be back soon with your dinner. Is there anything else I can do for you in the meantime?"

"You could get back to what you and Kate were about to do under that mistletoe before I so rudely barged in," Marla said with absolutely no shame. "For the second time today, mind you. My timing really is terrible, isn't it?"

"We weren't about to do anything."

"Sure, you weren't." Marla laughed but winced from the jostling movement. She reached for her ankle. "Ouch. I really did a number this time."

"Mom, I know you don't want to hear it, but you need to learn to slow down. Cody and I could've taken care of the horses tonight if you would've just asked. It wouldn't've been an issue at all. You don't need to add more things to your already full plate."

"Deacon, the day I slow down is the day you put me in the ground. I like to stay busy. It keeps me right in the head."

Of course, he understood that. His father's unexpected death had rattled them all, his mother the most. He knew they'd each worked through and processed it differently over the years. For Marla, that meant diving headfirst into farm responsibilities by picking up where her husband had left off. She was right. Slowing down wasn't an option. Not for the long term, at least.

But Deacon would make certain she slowed down at least for the next few days. She wouldn't like it, but she wouldn't have a choice.

"I want your word that you'll try to let me and Cody take care of you. At least while your ankle's on the mend."

"I will *try*," she agreed, but it wasn't convincing. "But I can't promise it won't be met without a little grumbling on my end."

"I wouldn't expect anything less than ten complaints

per day," Deacon quipped, ready for the swat on his arm that his mother delivered in response to his remark. "Maybe twelve."

"Deacon Winters, show this old mama of yours a little respect."

"I respect you, Mom. More than you will ever know."

She flapped her hands, urging her son closer. "Come here and give me a hug. I sure could use one."

Even though he was a grown man, there was always safety, comfort, and unconditional love to be found in his mother's arms. This time, he sensed the embrace was more for her than it was meant for him, so he was sure to squeeze extra tightly. When he pulled back, he couldn't help but notice the sheen of tears welling in her eyes.

"I'm sorry." Marla swiped a finger under her nose and sniffed, scolding the unbidden tear away. "I really hate that this had to happen right in the middle of our busy season."

"Will you please stop apologizing?"

"I'm serious, Deacon. This injury throws a monkey wrench into our entire operation. We need all hands on deck during this holiday rush and now I've gone and done this." She motioned toward her propped up foot.

Deacon disagreed. "We'll figure things out. One step at a time. And right now, that first step is to get you upright so you can eat the dinner you spent all evening preparing. On three. One, two," he guided. "Three." He took hold of her elbow to swivel her into a sitting position.

Like two staffers at a bustling restaurant, Cody and Kate simultaneously entered the room and went to work getting Marla situated with her lap table and a heaping plate of all the best comfort foods, complete with a cloth napkin that Kate had tried—and failed—to fold into what Deacon could only assume was a swan. Or a donkey. It was really difficult to tell but the effort was valiant.

He could see in his mother's eyes that she disliked being waited upon, but she'd have to accept their help. He would make certain of it.

"Thank you all. Truly. I'm really going to try not to make myself a nuisance. You'll hardly even notice me."

"Please stop apologizing for something you had no control over."

"That familiar line sure sounds like something I would say," Marla said. "In fact, I think I *have* said that to you many times over the years."

That comment felt like a sharp jab in Deacon's side. His mother had used those same words, but the truth was, the situations he often apologized for were well within his control, like his skiing accident that resulted in a fractured collarbone and even worse off skis. And most recently, the broken stairs leading up to the barn loft. There was blame to place with that and it landed squarely upon Deacon's shoulders.

"I'm going to fix those stairs first thing in the morning." Deacon turned his attention toward Kate who had just taken a seat in the old leather recliner off to the side. "I'm so sorry, but I don't think you'll be able to get back up to the loft tonight. Not safely, at least."

A flash of apprehension crossed over Kate's face before she marshaled her features. "Oh, okay. That's fine, I can—"

"Bunk with me!" Marla completed the thought for her with a tangible giddiness that couldn't go unnoticed. "I've got Deacon's empty, old room down the hall that you can stay in. Plus, I could really use the extra set of ears. You know, in case I need any help in the middle of the night. Cody sleeps like a hibernating bear, so he's of no use to me. Wouldn't wake up even if a freight train came barreling through his room."

"I work hard and sleep hard." Cody's shoulders lifted to his ears. "What can I say?"

Kate still didn't seem completely onboard. "If you're sure it's not an inconvenience."

"I busted the only way to get up to your room and *you're* worried about being an inconvenience? Kate, dear, trust me. I'd feel much more comfortable with you staying in the main house tonight."

"I would, too," Deacon agreed. The thought of Kate in that rickety barn while the storm raged outside made him uneasy with concern. He even worried a little about the horses, but he knew they were blanketed and tucked safely into their stalls and would ride out the storm in relative comfort. This was going to be a bad one, and he wanted everyone safe, sound and accounted for.

"Then who am I to argue?" Kate finally said. "I'll find a way to thank you guys for your hospitality. One way or another"

Deacon grinned. "I think you already have."

"Yeah?" Kate's eyes slanted. "How so?"

Marla sniffed and Deacon noticed the same sharp aroma wafting from the kitchen. "In the form of two, slightly burnt apple pies," Marla said, winking. "That's how."

Kate lurched from the chair. "Oh no! The pies!"

KATE

"Knit one, purl one?"

"Knit one, purl two," Kate corrected. She glanced up from the busy needles and yarn in her hands to survey Marla's handiwork. It wasn't half-bad for a first time knitter. Sure, there were a few holes where the yarn didn't get pulled quite tight enough, and there were also few saggy portions right around the middle, but all in all, it was a noble first attempt. And the perfect activity for the woman who didn't seem to comprehend the meaning of relaxation.

They had finished up dinner an hour or so earlier. Deacon retreated to his cottage and Cody to his upstairs bedroom, leaving Kate and Marla to watch *It's a Wonderful Life* that aired on the same station as Kate's news show. She just loved that movie and knew by the time the credits rolled across the screen, she'd have a steady trail of tears streaming down her face. It didn't matter that she watched it every year. Those ringing bells and angel wings would always be the cue to release the waterworks.

Marla couldn't sit still, even with the movie playing. She'd fidgeted and fussed and when Kate had asked if she happened to have any yarn and knitting needles, the woman's face lit up like a brilliant Christmas display. "I do!" She'd tried to stand to retrieve the items in question, but Kate was quick with a look that challenged Marla to stay in place. "In the hope chest in the first bedroom down the hall. They were Grandma Kay's. Haven't been used in years and I'm not even sure if the yarn will hold up, but it should all be in there. That woman sure loved to knit. Made both the boys stockings when they were babies. I still have them."

"Did she ever teach you how?"

"To knit? Nah, I never had the patience for it." Marla had tossed her head back and forth. "Anything that requires sitting still for that long makes my skin start to itch."

"But I've seen you in your shop. Seems like you do okay in there for hours on end, no?"

"Only because I've got people to chat with. Inventory to restock. I don't do well with silence and idle hands. Not since Joe passed, at least."

Kate had already been moving across the room so she prayed the hiccup in her step wasn't visible at the mention of Joe's name. Deacon had opened up a little about his father, but this was her first time hearing Marla speak of the man. She couldn't fathom the deep heartache his void must have created in their lives. Kate had lost people she cared about, but never a family member and certainly not someone she'd loved enough to pledge her own life to. Marla's pain was substantial and real and Kate felt her heart break a little for the woman who she'd only known a few days.

She had pondered that reality while she made her way into the spare bedroom and located the knitting supplies that were right where Marla had said they would be. There was something special about the Winters family. Kate had worked with other families before, but none had opened their arms—and their hearts—so fully. It was no secret Kate was falling for Deacon. It was nearly impossible not to. But she also found herself falling for Marla's warm, motherly nature and her go-getter attitude. For Cody's sarcastic wit and goofy, younger brother demeanor.

Kate was falling for this entire place and everything wrapped up in it. She was falling for Yuletide Farm and she never wanted to leave.

"Knit one, purl two. Knit one, purl two." An hour into their knitting session, Marla continued whispering the words as her hands followed the instructions. She lowered her chin at Kate, her eyes angling above her reading glasses. "You sure I'm doing this right?"

"Yep. It's looking great, too."

"You don't need to lie, dear. My ego isn't that fragile." She mouthed the movements again, this time less distinct. "What exactly are we making?"

"A scarf. It's the easiest thing to start with and if there's a part you don't like, you can hide it when you wear it."

"Knit one, purl two." Fingers tangling, Marla let out

a little huff and unwound the string from her needles. "Do you mind me asking where you learned to knit? I don't want to sound ageist, but you aren't exactly in the demographic that usually takes to this sort of hobby."

"As with most of the things I've learned, it was *on the job*." Kate settled her needles and yarn to her lap and made air quotes around her words. "My first assignment, actually. I was working for a fisherman named Michael Swinson. His wife, Betty, was an avid knitter. She'd bring her little basket down to the dock each day and by the end of my shift, she'd have fashioned a fabulous new creation. It fascinated me. I was no good at fishing, but Betty taught me all I needed to know about knitting and I absolutely loved it."

"I think you get to lead the most fascinating life, Kate." Marla rested her needles on the couch cushion beside her and collected the television remote from the end table to click off the screen. The T.V. darkened, along with the room, save for the bronze glow of the dwindling fire in the stove. "Meeting new people everywhere you go. Learning new trades." She paused as she gave Kate a pressing look. "I imagine that would make it hard to ever want to settle down."

"I've been doing this for seven years now, so it's all I really know. But I always told myself these assignments are a bit like job interviews, just in reverse. I'm the one deciding if I'm the right fit for the job, not the other way around."

"And how do you think you fit in here at the farm?"

"Well, I'm lousy at hauling trees and I'm not so sure

I'm cut out for storms like this one tonight, but the truth is, I've never felt more at home."

Marla regarded Kate with a look that reiterated everything Kate's heart felt in that moment. It was as though her soul was looking into a mirror. "I'm glad to hear it." The woman picked up her needles and began knitting once more. "Very glad to hear it."

WIND HOWLED AGAINST THE SHUTTERS, FLAPPING THE wooden slats like flags whipping up in a stormy gale. Kate couldn't sleep. She'd completed her scarf, helped Marla finish hers, and retreated to bed just a few strokes after midnight. She seldom had an issue falling asleep in a new place. In truth, her biggest bouts of insomnia often took place within her own apartment walls. At times, that place felt akin to an impersonal, rental hotel room. There was no identifying mark that made it hers. No monogramed towels. No custom curtains. She didn't even really like the comforter that draped over her own bed. She'd picked out one that looked similar to the quilt she remembered from the model home she had viewed before purchasing the place. It matched well with the paint. But it didn't feel like it belonged to her. She could sell it all tomorrow—her home and everything within it —and not even have the slightest twinge of remorse.

How was it, then, that she felt a tug in her stomach each time she thought of leaving Yuletide Farm? These memories that coated the walls in the forms of pictures, wallpapers, and paints weren't even hers. They belonged to a family that she'd merely inserted herself into.

When she'd tossed and turned enough to dizzy herself, Kate gave in and got up. Knitting always seemed to calm her, those trance-like, repetitive motions often enough to make her eyelids heavy and her mind equally drowsy. Crawling across the mattress toward the foot of the bed, Kate lifted the lid of the hope chest to rifle through the balls of yarn that she knew to be there. They had made scarves of rich, bold holiday colors earlier, so this time she pulled out all of the pastel skeins she could find. Just as she was reaching for a bundle of pale pink yarn, something else caught her eye.

The Winters Family.

The letters were stamped in gold across the leather-bound book. Kate pushed everything else aside and lifted the thick album from the trunk before working her way back up to the headboard to sit cross-legged. She flicked the nightstand lamp on and opened it up.

The black and white images looked like something out of a history book. Worn, weathered faces with hollow eyes stared back at her. Smiles were hard to detect, likely because they were hard to produce in that era. These were the images of early Californians who risked life and limb to settle this land. The tired stares that graced image after image made Kate's spirit heavy, like an anchor tugging her soul. She knew nothing of this sort of rugged and rough existence, nothing of the struggles some ancestors endured to secure an abundant life for their future generations.

With each turn of the page, Kate could sense an

upturn in spirit. Corners of mouths curved upward—if only slightly—a detectable joy now spread across the faces of children and parents alike. She read the notes scribbled in the margins listing the names and ages of each person within the frame. By the time the photographs morphed from grayscale to color, Kate started to recognize the subjects. Cody as a little boy, bundled in a puffy blue jacket while he held his Grandpa Tuff's big paw of a hand. There were images of a young Marla, her hair a brilliant red luster that evidently had faded to silver only in recent years. In many of the shots, she looked on from the periphery, tucked under the loving and possessive arm of a man Kate could only assume was her husband, Joe. He shared Deacon's large physique and matched with a twin twinkle in his chocolate colored eyes.

Her favorite image was of Deacon perched atop a pony, cowboy hat on his head and red boots snug on his feet. Kate smiled at the sweet thought of a young Deacon sleeping with those very boots on.

As the years passed, images of Deacon and Cody took center stage. They were rough and tumble teenagers with wild hair and brawny frames. It was hard to find a photograph without a tree in it—most often they were hoisted high upon shoulders as a show of brute strength. Kate paused at the next picture. It was of the three men—Deacon, Cody, and their father. There was nothing special about the image, nothing noteworthy in their poses or backdrop, but the look of love inscribed on each individual face was enough to make Kate's heart ache. Joe Winters stood in the center, his arms wrapped around his boys, pride filling his eyes. Deacon was young here, and when Kate turned the page and was met with a photograph of Deacon and Cody dressed in suits of black, eyes melancholy and expressions vapid, she nearly gasped.

He was so young. A boy. But in that image, she knew he had become a man and it appeared as though the weight of the farm and his family now rested squarely upon his shoulders.

It wasn't until a brunette entered the photographs some five or so years later that a smile finally returned to Deacon's face. It was barely perceptible at first, just a small, slight tip of his lips. But soon, his full-fledged grin was the only thing Kate could see. It was a magnet that pulled her into each picture and produced a similar one on her own face just in viewing it. Deacon's joy was palpable, and Kate figured the woman next to him had a little something to do with that.

There were images of the couple riding horses side-by-side through snowy mountain trails. Photographs where they were decked out in ski gear, poles gripped in their hands and eyes smiling under tinted goggles. Pictures of holidays and family celebrations and dinners so delectable it made Kate's taste buds tingle. But the image that stole her breath was the one with Deacon dropped down on one knee, a sparkling diamond ring pinched between his fingers, and an elated smile plastered on the young woman's face.

This was Jenny. It had to be.

Kate had already spent some time pondering Deacon's situation. She assumed Jenny was someone important. But it was also clear that his heart had been broken. Shattered. Part of Kate had wondered if Jenny had failed to reciprocate Deacon's affection—if he'd proposed and she'd declined. But this picture was evidence to the contrary. It was clear the woman had said yes. Enthusiastically, too, it appeared.

So what led to this hesitant, sometimes sullen and guarded new version of Deacon?

Kate hated to think of the possibilities, and when her head kept circling back to the same speculation, she had to close the album, stow it away, and turn off the lights and her thoughts. It was just too painful to go there.

One thing she knew for sure: Deacon Winters was no stranger to loss, both in life and in love.

DEACON

Deacon took another guzzle of his woefully tepid coffee. Unlike the lone mug housed in his cupboard at the cottage, his mother had enough to use a different one each day of the month if she so desired. It appeared she had kept every single cup she'd acquired throughout her lifetime. Every Mother's Day gift and birthday present. Every failed masterpiece from her sons' ceramic classes. Deacon wasn't sure why that was always their go-to when it came to gift giving. Apparently, he and Cody weren't all that creative, as evidenced by the three mugs that had some version of *World's Best Mom* printed across the side.

The current mug Deacon drank his weak, medium roast blend from was festive with glittering white snowflakes stamped on the border and a little spotted deer with snow-tipped antlers embossed on the façade. Sure, it was unquestionably feminine, but it held his coffee fine and that's all he really cared about.

He had spent the first hour of daylight sipping from the mug and scrolling through Kate's online footage of their farm. There was the rental tree drop-off and wreath making with his mother. Interviews with bright-eyed children detailing each item scrawled on holiday wish lists they'd shipped off to the North Pole. Kate had even created a short segment she'd titled, *"Find That Tree!"* where she challenged three separate families in a race to search for, cut down, and haul off their perfect Christmas tree. The winner received a twenty-dollar gift certificate to the farm store to purchase decorations for their new evergreen possession, which struck Deacon as a brilliant idea.

And she had done it all on her own. Without a camera man. Without a producer. Just Kate, her phone, and her charisma. Based on the comments, she didn't need those other elements. Her audience loved the bonus piece on Marla's infamous hot chocolate, and at the end of the video, Kate asked viewers to leave their own holiday drink recipes in the section below. Deacon was shocked by the amount of interaction that post received. There were hundreds of responses. What stunned him even more was that Kate took the time to reply to them all. Sometimes it was just a thumbs up, but she made sure to acknowledge each comment and he knew that was intentional on her part. She was just like that.

"Morning."

Deacon startled at the live version of the recorded voice he had been listening to for the last hour.

Kate meandered into the room with bleary, half-lidded eyes, wearing one of his old high school t-shirts paired with faded sweatpants. The ensemble hung loose and was ill-fitting, but she looked adorable all the same. She pushed a fist to her eyes and rubbed, then yawned as she stretched her arms skyward like a cat arching its back after a long winter's nap. When she dropped her arms back down, she met Deacon's gaze and smiled lazily. "You're up awfully early."

"I'm heading out soon to do some shoveling before we open things up."

Her eyes flicked over her shoulder toward the wood paned window at her back. "Oh, gosh. I didn't even think about that. These big storms create a lot of work for you when they blow through, don't they?"

Deacon shrugged. "A fair amount. Luckily, the snow plow comes through before sunup to clear out the roadways so people can actually get to the tree farm. I know the owner of the company so I always throw a little extra money his way so he'll clear out the parking lot for me, too. All I really have to do is make sure all the walking paths are safe and that we haven't lost any trees overnight. I'm headed out on the snowmobiles in a few minutes to do just that."

"Do you mind if I come with you?"

"To look for downed trees?"

"Yeah." She slumped against the pale yellow farm-house wall and yawned again, sleep still lingering in her eyes. "I've never ridden on a snowmobile before."

"No? I don't know why, but I'm a little surprised to learn that."

"Probably because I've ridden camels, rickshaws, and even dolphins. But not a snowmobile. Go figure."

Deacon collected his mug from the table, shoved his cell phone into his jacket pocket, and pushed to his feet. "You're more than welcome to join me. They're relatively straightforward to drive so I don't think you should have any problem—"

"Oh." She shook her head so rapidly her messy bun flopped back and forth. "I don't think I want to drive one. I was hoping maybe I could just ride on yours with you." She paused, then added in a rush, "But only if that's okay."

Deacon coughed and instantly felt the acidic bite of his coffee repeating on him. With one balled up fist, he thrust twice against his chest and swallowed so loudly it came out as a gulp. "Sure. I mean, yeah. That's totally fine."

"Great! Just give me five minutes to get ready and I'll meet you back down here."

"How about I grab the snowmobile from the storage barn and swing back around to pick you up? That way you don't have to walk all the way down in the snow. There's a lot of it."

"That would be really nice, Deacon. Thank you. I'll be quick. Promise."

As Kate scampered down the hall, Deacon downed the remaining sludge in his mug, rinsed it clean in the sink, and headed out the back door to set out for the barn. If he hadn't been fully awake at that point, the bone-chilling cold that rushed over the apples of his cheeks would've shocked him into complete alertness. The temperatures had dropped by double-digits overnight. With the collar of his insulated jacket flipped up to shield his neck against the icy blast and his work gloves fitted to his hands, Deacon stepped off the back porch stoop, letting each boot sink slowly into the pristine covering of white until he couldn't see his toes and snow came clear up to his shins.

This was angel making sort of snow. Light. Powdery. The kind so soft one could fall back into it and feel as though they would never fully land. Funny. That was the same way Deacon felt when it came to Kate.

What had this woman done to him?

Even if he had all the time in the world to sort through possible reasons for this almost ethereal feeling, he figured he would never arrive at an answer that made any real sense. Some things just couldn't be explained. Like how Santa's magical sleigh could carry enough presents for the world's population of little boys and girls. Or how fruitcake ever earned its way into the ranks of holiday treats. Or most puzzling, how his shattered heart somehow felt—for the first time in years—like it was in the process of being put back together again.

Deacon forced those thoughts from his head while he removed the battered canvas covering from the snowmobile inside the barn and fired up the engine. This thing with Kate didn't need to be analyzed. He also didn't dwell too long on the fact that she'd asked to ride double. If he gave that another thought, his stomach would tangle with nerves that just might twist him into immobility. Before he could chicken out, he nudged a helmet onto his head, grabbed another for Kate, and angled the mobile out of the barn to double back toward the house. The blades underneath the small vehicle carved ruts into the snow, curving and bending with the fresh mountain terrain in parallel lines. As he eased up the hill, he couldn't squelch the chuckle that rumbled his chest at the sight of Kate waiting for him, bundled in a rust-colored coat she must've retrieved from the depths of his mother's hall closet. Her thumb jutted out in a hitchhiker's signal and she danced in place in what Deacon assumed was an attempt to maintain warmth. It was glaringly off-beat yet endearing all the same.

"Hey there, handsome," she said with a lash-fluttering wink. "Got room for one more?"

"Hop on." Deacon passed off the extra helmet and waited while Kate maneuvered it onto her head before settling onto the back of the snowmobile. When her arms wove around his waist and her hands clasped at his middle like a makeshift seatbelt, he revved the vehicle and set out down the hillside before she had time to change her mind.

"What are we looking for, exactly?" Kate shouted over the grating motor that buzzed beneath them like an angry chainsaw.

"Any possible damage the storm might've caused overnight." Deacon tilted his head back so she could hear him more clearly. "Fallen trees or branches. Things of that nature."

"Like that?" Kate nudged her chin and set her eyes forward.

Deacon groaned. "*Exactly* like that."

Up ahead, one of their largest firs rested horizontally across their path as a massive evergreen barricade. When Deacon eased up to it, he could see the many branches crunched and snapped beneath the substantial weight of the tree.

"Can it be salvaged?"

Deacon swung his leg over the mobile and stepped closer to gain a better vantage point to assess the damage. "Not as a tree that anyone will want to display in their home, unfortunately. But we can save some of these branches to use for garland and wreaths. And we'll chop up the trunk for firewood. It won't be a complete waste. But shoot, that was a really good-looking tree."

He pulled a walkie-talkie from his belt loop and called up Cody to give him the coordinates of their find. It would need to be their first order of business that morning. With the farm opening in just a few short hours, they would have to work quickly. But Cody was a pro at this sort of thing and if Deacon had to guess, his brother secretly enjoyed firing up the saw and having at it.

For the next fifteen minutes, Deacon and Kate zipped in and out of the rows, needles of emerald blurring in their periphery as they sped past. After their first discovery, Deacon had prepared for a slew of more just like it, but much to his relief, they didn't encounter anything other than a broken limb or two. The night's gusts and gales proved no match for the sturdy roots and trunks of the good majority of their Yuletide trees and for that, he was overwhelmingly grateful.

"Let's make a quick run through the rentals and then we can head on in."

Kate nodded. Her arms hugged firmly around Deacon's middle and when he skirted a tree a touch faster than necessary, making the back of the mobile wobble and wave like a fan, that secure grasp squeezed even tighter.

"Sorry about that," Deacon apologized, even though he wasn't sorry one little bit. He'd fishtail around every bend if it meant having Kate's hands on him like this. The only thing better would be if things were reversed and he had her in his arms. He suddenly got an idea. "Any chance you want to drive?"

"The snowmobile?" Kate shouted her incredulity.

"Yes, the snowmobile." Decelerating, he slowed to an idle to give Kate a bit of quiet to mull over the proposition. "It's easy. You'll do great."

"Or I could take out every tree with my wild and erratic driving."

"If you do, I'll just send the bill to your station." Before she could protest, Deacon slid off the seat and moved behind her, giving her shoulder a small bump. "Go on. Scooch forward." He waited while Kate shimmied up and hovered her palms above the steering handles like they just might burn her if she actually touched them. "Go easy on the throttle and if you need to stop suddenly for any reason, you can always push this button as a last resort."

Kate studied the kill switch, drew in a shoulder-lifting breath, and affirmed her confidence with a nod. "Okay. I've got this."

"You totally do."

Taking position, Deacon moved forward until his chest pressed solidly against Kate's back.

"Wait?"

He withdrew a sliver. "Yeah?"

"Would you mind…?" Her hand went to her coat and when she retrieved her phone, Deacon hissed out his worried breath and snuggled in close again. "Would you mind filming this?"

"Right. Of course. No problem."

With his arm stretched to full length in front of them, Deacon balanced the phone in his large hand and hit record.

Kate hit the gas.

The snowmobile pitched headlong at breakneck speed, like a smooth rock released from the building tension of a drawn slingshot.

"Wahoo!" A shout of unadulterated joy tore from Kate's lips the instant the vehicle took off down the mountainside. "Is this too fast? Am I going too fast? Should I slow down? Are we going to crash?"

"Nope. Not at all. You're doing fine. Just keep doing what you're doing."

Deacon loved that he could see Kate's face reflected on the screen of her phone as it recorded their downhill ride. Pure glee set her eyes wildly alight and the smile she beamed rivaled a child given a brand new puppy on Christmas morning. Gold-spun strands of hair that peeked out from beneath her helmet coiled and twisted around her face and her cheeks pinked as the frigid wind whisked over her ivory skin. She was beautiful, carefree, and the very best vision Deacon had ever seen.

"This is a-*mazing*!" Kate squealed around a continuous giggle she couldn't contain. "I love this!"

Deacon's heart did a double take at those words. He loved this, too. Maybe he loved more than just this.

Before he could reprimand his wayward thoughts and shove them into time-out where they belonged, the cell phone in his grip pulsed, their mirror images suddenly replaced by an incoming call as the name *Courtney Druthers* flashed across the top like a lit-up marquee.

"I think you're getting a call." Deacon spoke into the shell of Kate's ear but the motor rumbled louder than his volume.

"I'm getting a what?"

"You're getting a call!"

Kate released her hand from the throttle and the snowmobile backed off in speed so rapidly it nearly felt as though they were sent into reverse. Her body slammed back into Deacon's chest right as the phone tumbled from his hand to the packed snow below.

"Oof!" Kate's breath rushed, the wind knocking straight out of her. "Sorry about that. I should've practiced stopping before I set out speeding."

"I'm not sorry." Deacon pulled her in close.

Kate slowly turned her head to cast a look over her shoulder and if they weren't wearing these cumbersome helmets, Deacon would've kissed her. Everything within him begged to and everything on her face reiterated that desire. The moment was primed and perfect for it.

192 | MEGAN SQUIRES

"I...uh..." Kate suddenly swung back and lifted the helmet off before shaking her head like a dog after a bath. The faint smell of apples wafting from her long tresses had Deacon even more dizzied than before, something he didn't deem possible. What kind of spell did she have on him? "My phone. Where'd it go? You said I was getting a call?"

"Oh. Yeah." He reached down and scooped the device from the snow, brushing off the icy clumps before passing it to her. "Sorry, I dropped it when we stopped so suddenly."

"That was completely my fault. I think I could use a few more hours behind the wheel before I consider myself even remotely proficient."

"I can arrange for that, if you like."

Hiking a leg over the seat, Kate got off the snowmobile and strode a few feet away, her boots leaving alternating tracks in the virgin snow as she paced circles around Deacon and the vehicle. "Nah. I think I'll leave the driving to you from now on." She lifted the phone high like a beacon, eyes squinted heavenward under a crumpled brow. "No cell service out here, huh?"

"Sorry. It's a bit spotty this far out. Do you think the call was important?"

"Hard to say, but it was from my boss."

Deacon didn't know why his stomach dropped upon hearing that. Of course, he hadn't forgotten that Kate's very presence on the farm was all part of her job. He was well aware of the fact that her time at Yuletide was limited. Yet he'd somehow packed up and pushed that reality off to the side to deal with at a later date. Prefer-ably next calendar year.

"Is it okay if we head home so I can call her back? Or at least find somewhere with decent reception? I probably shouldn't leave her waiting too long. The word patience doesn't really exist in Courtney Druther's vocabulary and I don't think it would fair well for my paycheck if I'm the first to teach it to her."

"Sounds like a gem."

"She's honestly not all that bad," Kate said, giving the woman the benefit of the doubt, but only for a moment before she tacked on, "But she's not all that good, either." Returning to her position at the rear of the snowmobile, Kate dropped her chin onto Deacon's shoulder and made his already erratic heartbeat quicken when she uttered, "You're a much better boss. The best one yet."

KATE

"Pick up…Pick *up*," Kate hissed into the receiver in time with the unanswered ring that pulsed every three seconds like a steady, sluggish metronome. Courtney's voicemail sounded urgent. At least the words Kate could decipher from the bouts of spotty dialogue seemed urgent.

It would not bode well for Kate's future at the news station to leave her boss hanging like this. Not when things already felt so unorthodox, uncertain, and downright weird. A few months back, a mere thirty minutes had lapsed between Courtney's text and Kate's reply, which resulted in donut deprivation in the staff room for a full week following that isolated slip-up. Sure, Kate couldn't confirm that the two scenarios were linked, but the fact that Courtney would always grab the very last apple fritter just seconds before Kate could make a move for it made the absurd gesture seem entirely plausible. She'd finally gotten past that silly passive-aggressive donut episode. What would she face this time around, now that Courtney's call remained unreturned going on three hours?

Kate dropped her head back onto the couch cushion and exhaled a strangled breath that lifted the wisps of hair framing her face. Today was shaping up to be a doozy. And then there was that near-kiss with Deacon. It was hard to even call it that because it wasn't like he'd made a move or anything. But if they both didn't look like space-bound astronauts, what with those ungainly helmets keeping them behind plastic and polycarbonate, she was certain they would've kissed. It was one of those situations where she could feel it everywhere. Her ears that rung like silver sleigh bells. The percussion of her heart that outpaced anything the Little Drummer Boy could crank out. Her palms that sweat and her legs that tingled. The moment was a full body one—every part aside from her lips that should've been pressed to Deacon's.

Courtney Druthers was a buzzkill and Kate grew exponentially aggravated each time she tried—and failed—to reach her.

Tossing her useless phone to the couch, Kate studied the stark white sheet of falling snow that swathed the forest line outside the window. Deacon and Cody had made the call to shut down the farm for the day. Despite the morning's snow removal, nearby roads were now closed and the white-out conditions weren't exactly ideal for tree cutting. This was a *tuck-yourself -inside-with-a-good-book* sort of day, but Kate couldn't even do *that* because the one novel she did bring with her was stowed away in her overnight bag currently trapped in the barn loft she couldn't access.

The day was a waste and while it wasn't in Kate's nature to accept defeat without a proper fight, she waved her proverbial white flag and wrote it off as a total loss. It didn't help that Deacon was down at the horse barn with his brother and Joshua, all hands on deck to secure and repair the decimated staircase. Kate would have gladly perched on a nearby hay bale, posting up by the men at work while she had Courtney's number on repeat. But that particular part of the barn was a cell phone dead zone and Kate knew the best use of time would be spent in the main house, making sure Marla was taken care of and staying off that sprained ankle.

But the woman was stubborn and each time Kate offered to fold a load of freshly laundered clothes, grab a cold beverage from the fridge, or put on another track of Christmas carols, it was met with an eye roll and a frustrated, sputtering lip.

"I don't need a maid, Kate." Marla's hands went to her waist in defiance. "I can do these things on my own."

"I'm sure you *can.* But you *shouldn't.*" It was admittedly tiring, this back and forth of matching wills. "Deacon's not going to like it if he walks in to see you standing on that injured foot, Marla. I just got on his good side. Please don't put me back on his bad one."

"Oh, sweetie. You were never on that man's bad side. There's only been one woman to cross into that territory, and suffice it to say, she's *long* gone."

Kate bristled. That was no way to talk about a woman six feet in the grave. Any other day, Kate wouldn't have poked her nose so deeply into business that was not hers, but this day was different. Maybe it was the unpredictability of the weather which vacillated between sunny and stormy like the flip of a switch. Maybe it was the fact that she couldn't get ahold of her boss and her mounting frustration opted to find another place for release. Whatever it was, Kate didn't hold back.

"Listen, I get that Jenny broke Deacon's heart, I do. But it's not right to talk about someone who clearly isn't here to defend herself. Someone who *can't* defend herself, even if she wanted to."

Marla dropped into the wingback chair next to the couch and hoisted her bum ankle onto a brocade ottoman, then gave Kate the most peculiar look. "What makes you think Jenny can't defend herself?"

"Oh, I don't know." Kate tossed her hands into the air like she was throwing a pizza. "Maybe because she's dead?"

If someone had told Marla she just grew elf ears, she couldn't have looked more surprised. That fresh shock quickly turned humorous when she unleashed a fit of laughter that had Kate plastered up against the back of the couch from the shear, uproarious impact of it. "Jenny's not dead, Kate."

"She's not?"

Wiping the tip of her nose and shaking her head, tears streaming down her face as she continued in her bout of hilarity, Marla said, "Goodness, no. Jenny is alive and well, to the best of my knowledge, at least."

"I just assumed…"

"That no living, breathing woman would willingly leave a man like Deacon?"

Kate wasn't sure that was totally what she meant, but close. "I guess so. I mean, the way he won't let people talk about her. How he cuts off any conversation that might bring up her name. I don't know." She shrugged. "I just figured she had to be *gone*-gone. It was like he was protecting her memory or something."

"I think what Deacon is trying to do is protect his heart." A chiming bell from the kitchen punctuated the end of her sentence, and when Marla leaned forward to rise from her chair, Kate stood first.

"Nope. You stay put." She waggled a finger at Marla. "I'll see to it. What do you have a timer set for, anyway?"

"Just a batch of sugar cookies I whipped up. Grandma Kay's recipe. I thought it might be fun to decorate them this evening once Joshua and the boys get back from fixing the staircase."

"Marla! You're not supposed to do anything that requires you to be on your feet! I'm fairly certain baking falls into that category." Kate tightened her brow while giving her best pout, trying to put the woman in her place but failing. "When did you even have time to do this without me catching you?"

"When you were in the shower right after you came back from snowmobiling."

"Sneaky woman." Before Kate had retreated to the

guest bath to take a nice, warm shower in an attempt to defrost, she had passed through the family room only to spy Marla sound asleep on the couch, a crackling fire that dwindled to embers serving as her afternoon lullaby. She'd been in that precise place when Kate had returned, too. "Deacon's not going to be happy."

"We'll just tell him you made them."

"The only way he'll believe that is if they're burnt, broken or otherwise completely ruined."

"Well, you keep stalling and they just might be. Go on and get those puppies out of the oven before my snowmen cookies look like they spent a day at the beach without sunscreen."

Kate snickered as she followed her nose into the nearby kitchen. The entire space smelled of sugary goodness and she sincerely doubted the kitchen of Mrs. Claus herself could even compare. There was that sweet, buttery scent of freshly baked cookies that translated into the warmest feeling of love. Kate imagined Deacon and Cody as young boys, bounding through the back door after school, backpacks slung on their shoulders while they raced around the butcher block island to steal a treat before properly washing their hands. She just knew Marla was the type of mother to have after-school goodies waiting for her sons.

"Did they burn?"

Marla's holler from the adjacent room tugged Kate out of her daydream and back onto the task at hand. Opening the oven door, she let the rich aroma mixed with heat rush over her skin before she located the mitts to pull the cookies from their racks.

"Nope. They're perfect!" Kate called back. She hip-bumped the oven door into place. "Which means we'll never be able to trick Deacon into believing I did this."

"Believing you did what?"

Kate whirled around, sending several snowmen flying from the baking sheets. Before they hit the ground, Cody lurched forward to rescue the airborne cookies, snatching them right out of the sky like a major league baseball player catching a pop fly.

"Grandma Kay's sugar cookies!" He cried appreciatively as he chomped the head off one.

"You're not supposed to eat them before they're decorated," Marla reprimanded. She hobbled into the kitchen, holding onto the ledge of the counter for balance while Cody, Deacon, and Joshua filtered into the small space, bringing a rush of winter wind that chased them through the back door.

"And you're not supposed to be on your feet, Mom." Deacon nudged the door shut and then unwound the scarf from his neck to ball it between his hands. He shook it at her, but the floppy green and red fringe did little to help assert his demand. "Why would you feel the need to bake when you're supposed to be resting? Don't you want to get better?"

"Oh, I didn't bake these. Kate did."

"Yeah, for some strange reason, I'm not buying that."

The devilish lift to Deacon's mouth and his sidelong glance had every bit of Kate heating up. Most noticeably her hands. She looked down at the sheet still gripped between her fingers and suddenly realized the metal had started to burn right through the padded mitts, singeing her skin with growing intensity. Without thinking, she tossed the tray onto the counter.

"Acck!" She yanked off the mitts and sprinted to the sink to flip the lever to the coldest water possible. It stung initially, but eased into relief once her palms adjusted to the shocking variance in temperatures. Sighing, she let the liquid rush over her reddened palms.

"Are you okay?" Deacon was at her side in a blink. "You didn't get burned, did you?"

"I'm fine." Kate slumped forward against the sink basin. The scorched sensation subsided quickly and the bright red of her palms had thankfully started to fade to pale pink. "Just held onto that sheet for a bit too long and it got a little hot."

"Too many cooks in the kitchen!" Marla shuffled toward Joshua and Cody, swatting her hands to shoo them along and into the family room. "Let's let Kate and Deacon finish up in here on their own. They don't need us milling about and getting in the way."

Kate didn't have to look to confirm Marla's eyes on the sprig of greenery dangling directly above them.

Joshua stole a handful of cookies before trailing the others out of the kitchen, but not before he shot Deacon a wink of encouragement that had Kate suddenly flushed with nerves. Between her heated palms and her fuzzy brain, her entire body had gone utterly haywire.

"What was that all about?" Deacon tore off a section from the paper towel roll and passed it to Kate. He stood by, arms woven across his chest as she dried her hands.

"Umm." Kate eased her gaze toward the ceiling.

"Oh." Deacon jumped out from under the spray of green. "I'd forgotten that was there…"

"Yeah. Same."

They stared at one another, immobilized like two frozen ice sculptures.

"Your mom is sort of relentless," Kate teased.

"That, she is." Deacon chuckled, but it was nervous laughter, not the genuine sound she grown used to hearing from him lately.

"Do you think maybe we should just give in?" Kate's finger wound in the paper towel, wringing it until she could feel her pulse beating in just the tip.

"Give in?" He took a step toward her. "As in…?"

She paused. "As in, maybe we should just kiss and get it over with."

A look of shear disappointment moved across Deacon's face, causing insecurity to sweep through Kate's belly. Evidently, they weren't together in that same line of thinking. She could have sworn they were both talking about the silly mistletoe that teased and tormented them to no end.

"Kate Carmichael." Deacon moved even closer still. Kate retreated, surprised by his sudden advancement. Her backside collided with the counter. Trapped there, Deacon's body was nearly flush with hers and his arms bracketed on either side, hands gripping the tile, locking her in. Their faces aligned and when he parted his lips to speak, she could feel the warmth of his cinnamon tinged breath rush across her mouth. "When I do finally kiss you, it's not going to be something that I just want to get over with."

"Oh." All of Kate's air left her in a whoosh.

"I want to take my time. I hope that's okay with you."

She nodded, a bunch of little nervous nods in a row. "Yeah, that's definitely okay."

"Good." He smirked before he pushed off the counter. "Just wanted to make sure we were on the same page."

"Same page." Kate couldn't collect herself. She was as dizzied as a spinning top about to teeter over. "Totally same page."

DEACON

He'd had two clear opportunities to kiss the woman of his dreams and passed them both up. What sort of man did that? *A man who doesn't know the first thing about falling in love,* Deacon thought to himself as he sat deeply in the driver's seat, the sharp flare of sun forcing him to squint into the rays that flooded his truck cab with brilliant, morning light. He'd been so frustrated with himself that he almost overlooked the mountain beauty around him, focusing instead on the movie real of memories from the night prior. The night where Kate had suggested they kiss and he—like the fool he evidently was—said something along the lines of, "Not now, thanks."

His grip on the steering wheel tightened. Why couldn't he be a "seize the day" sort of guy, like the one who had the boldness to ask Kate out in his mother's farm store, with an audience, no less? In another life, Deacon could be that man. In fact, even in *this* life he could've been him. All he would have to do is rewind five years and erase the one relationship that made him question everything about love, his farm, and his future.

But life didn't come with a remote. You couldn't rewind. You couldn't pause. And you certainly couldn't fast forward. Deacon had tried and failed too many times at that. Life was meant to be lived and felt. Every minute, every second.

Deacon's emotions fell in step with his thoughts as a fresh wave of regret swept through him. Why did he feel like Kate was already fifty miles down the highway, headed in the opposite direction? He couldn't let her go that easily, not without telling her what she meant to him. In that very moment, just as he flipped his turn signal on and coasted into the lot of Al's Grocery, he made a vow that before the sun slipped behind the mile-high trees on his property nearing day's end, he would make his feelings known. One way or another.

Just that bit of resolve added a pep to Deacon's step that had vanished in recent years. It felt good to have a plan. He strolled the cart up and down the aisles of the quaint store, feeling lighter than he had in a long while, and he hummed along with the instrumental score of Christmas carols that ran faintly in the background. To his delight, there was a display of discounted Santa hats at an end cap and he collected a handful for the crew back home, shoving one onto his head to wear while he scoped out the items on his list.

Chicken pot pie, no peas. That was the menu for tonight. He'd spent a generous amount of time combing through internet recipes and landed on one that looked similar to the dish served at the restaurant they'd frequented that week. It didn't take long to locate the ingredients he needed for the meal, but before Deacon meandered his way to the checkout stand with his bounty, he took a turn down the wine aisle to peruse the small section of bottled beverages. He rarely drank, but he knew from Kate's sommelier episode that she often enjoyed relaxing with an after dinner glass. But choosing the appropriate one—even from the limited mountain store selection—was not in Deacon's wheelhouse. He stood there, gaze blank and knowledge nonexistent, playing a game of eenie, meenie, minie mo with the four nearest bottles.

"Need some help?"

The voice at his back made all of the hairs on Deacon's neck stand on end, like the wary hackles on a threatened dog. He whipped around and the fluffy, dangling ball at the tip of his cap smacked him right in the eye. Even with the now blurry vision, Deacon could make out the woman before him as plain as day. His stomach lurched.

"Jenny?"

"Deacon?" Her eyes rounded in matching surprise. "I didn't realize it was…I didn't know that was you," she stammered as she flapped her ski gloves against her palm, her feet shuffling on the ground, shaking off loose little bits of unmelted snow she'd tracked inside. "The hat and all. Not your typical cowboy one."

She flicked a finger toward the felt cap. Deacon swiped it from his head and tossed it into the cart. "It's my winter disguise," he said, feeling more stupid than ever. "What are you doing here?"

"Grocery shopping," she answered. Evidently sarcasm was still her trusty go-to.

"I mean here, as in the Sierras."

"I've been back for a while now, Deacon." The funny look she gave him made Deacon feel like he was missing something. He probably was. But when things had ended between them, he'd pledged never to look Jenny up. He made it a rule not to follow her on social media. He didn't text her on lonely nights when he wondered if they could've made things work had they just given it another shot. He did not wish to turn into one of those pathetic guys who followed their ex's every move, always keeping tabs and never really cutting ties.

No, with Jenny it had been a clean break, both with his heart and their relationship.

She stepped closer to the wall of wine. "I'd go with the 2017 Cabernet. Oaky with hints of black cherry and hazelnut. It's my favorite. Warm and spicy. The perfect winter wine."

The price tag on the suggested bottle sure fit the bill when it came to Jenny and her lavish tastes. Deacon stooped down and grasped the neck of the bottle directly beneath it, not even bothering to look at the blend, vintage, or cost. "This is the one I was actually looking for." He swung the wine bottle between them like a pendulum before placing it into his filled cart. "I should head to the checkout stand. I've got a tub of whipped cream in the cart and don't want it to melt."

Jenny nodded but there was something strained behind her gaze he couldn't quite interpret. "It's good to see you, Deacon." She smiled but it didn't lift high enough to touch the corners of her eyes. "I've thought a lot about you over the years and always kind of hoped we'd run into one another like this. I guess it's serendipity."

"It's something," Deacon muttered. He wasn't about to get pulled into a painful session of reminiscing about the 'good ol' days' with Jenny. He had no room in his head or his heart for that right now. "Take care, Jen. Merry Christmas."

Before he could process what was happening, Jenny marched forward and wrapped Deacon in a startling hug. His straight arms were pinned at his sides as she constricted him with a squeeze that felt close to suffocation.

"Merry Christmas, Deacon," she said with her face smashed against his chest. She pulled back quickly and tugged on the hem of her coat, readjusting her composure before adding, "Happy New Year to you, too."

"Still nothing?"

Deacon doubled at the waist to flip on the oven light, liking the sight of the flaky, golden texture on the rising crust of his pot pies. The hearty aroma alone was enough to make his stomach growl in anticipation. The fact that the pies looked as good as they smelled was just a pleasant added bonus.

Kate scooted out a barstool from underneath the

island and flopped down, expelling a breath with the motion. "I got another voicemail this afternoon," she said. She perched her elbows on the tiled counter and cupped her face in her hands. "At this point, we are playing the longest game of phone tag known to man."

"And you can't just text her?" Deacon adjusted the time on the stove, adding five more minutes to the countdown before rotating around to face Kate. Disappointment tugged at her typically happy expression and Deacon wished there was a way he could alleviate some of that frustration. He hoped the home cooked feast currently in the oven might take the edge off. A good meal usually did that for him, but he figured men and women were wired differently when it came to things of that nature.

"She says this information is too good to be typed out in a text. That it needs to be delivered over the phone."

"Well, that's promising, right?"

Kate waggled her shoulders. "Hard to say. Courtney's idea of good is all over the map, but I suppose that's to be expected in our line of work. I mean, for everyone else, a twenty car pile up on Interstate 80 is a disaster. At the very least, a huge traffic inconvenience. For us, it's five o'clock news."

"Fair point." Deacon hated how unsettled Kate had seemed since yesterday's missed call. She was a swirl of emotion, like a snow globe tipped upside-down and shaken about. "Hopefully you two can connect tonight."

"I sure hope so. I honestly don't think I can spend another night with all of this not knowing nonsense. I have half a mind to just drive myself down to the valley and show up at her door, demanding answers."

"I wouldn't recommend that." While it wasn't presently storming like it had been earlier in the day, roads would be slushy and black ice could be a very real threat. Even the most experienced driver would be challenged in these unsafe conditions.

"You're right." Kate twisted an errant strand of hair around her finger and screwed up her mouth into a pout. "Employees usually aren't in the best positions to demand much from their employers."

"I wasn't referring to that, but I do think that's a wise revelation. I just meant that I wouldn't recommend being out on the roads tonight, especially if you haven't driven in the snow much."

"Agreed. I guess that's something I should practice if I plan to make the drive back and forth from Sacramento more often. Maybe I can do an *On the Job* with that snow plow friend of yours. You think you could introduce us and possibly help line things up?"

She said it so casually, like it wasn't this perfect little gift she'd given him with her candid statement.

"You're planning to make the drive back and forth from Sacramento?" He repeated her exact words, as though somehow saying them in his own voice could aid in understanding their true meaning. It didn't work. He remained dumbfounded.

"Well, yeah." Kate stopped hair-twirling and leveled Deacon with a look that had his heart bottoming out. "I mean, how else am I going to see you once this job is over? I suppose I could get myself a sleigh and some magic reindeer that could fly me back and forth…"

Deacon didn't answer that, nor acknowledge her obvious joke, and the oven timer that suddenly trilled as her words trailed off nearly shot him sky high.

"Maybe I'm thinking too far ahead…" Kate slid off the stool and paced the kitchen to join Deacon. Like she'd lived there all her life, she opened the drawer next to the stove to locate another pair of mitts, slipped them on, and helped him pull the delectable pot pies from their racks.

"You're not. Thinking too far ahead, that is." Deacon had planned to have this conversation. In fact, he'd been ruminating on it all day long. He just didn't think Kate would be the one to broach it. Once again, she had caught him off guard in the very best way. "We'll make you a snow-savvy driver in no time, Kate Carmichael. That's a promise."

KATE

Chicken pot pie was entirely underrated. Maybe the idea of consuming chicken in pie form wasn't all that appealing for some, but to Kate, the meal she'd just devoured easily made it onto her list of top ten favorites. Admittedly, that might've had a little something to do with the man who prepared it for her.

When she came into the kitchen after filming a video for an idea she'd conjured up that afternoon about tree stands and how to select the right one, Kate unknowingly entered into a culinary explosion. Deacon had holiday jazz music cranked to full volume and he gleefully danced about the room like a man leading a partner. From her concealed vantage point in the hallway, Kate took in the show as he chopped, sliced, and seasoned each ingredient with such attention to detail it was as though he'd be graded on the final outcome. Thyme and black pepper went into a ceramic mixing bowl already containing premeasured amounts of flour, cream, and broth. Diced chicken and a medley of root vegetables boiled on the stove. The snap of onions sautéing in melting butter with minced garlic made Kate salivate on the spot. She could already taste the rich gravy that this combination of ingredients would create and she knew her dependable freezer meals would never again satisfy her hunger.

Embarrassment, followed by an unmistakable radiance of pride, had washed over Deacon's face when he lifted his eyes from his work and met Kate's shameless stare. That same pride grew exponentially throughout dinner, and each time Kate complimented the feast—which was after every bite she took—she could sense Deacon's appreciation swell within his chest.

He was detail oriented, not only in his ability to create such a delightful meal from scratch, but in the way he paid attention to the things many men might otherwise overlook. Kate had wavered on her dinner selection for just a moment at the restaurant and Deacon remembered. He had even committed to memory the fact that she didn't like peas. Sure, vegetables weren't often the subjects of great romances, but to Kate, these small, simple gestures meant everything.

Dusk had slipped into twilight and twilight into nightfall when Kate found herself at Deacon's side, their hands elbow deep in warm, sudsy sink water. One would scrub the plate, the other would rinse and settle it into the drying rack, and they repeated this process until each dish, pan, and pot was scoured clean. It was methodical, yet relaxing, in a way Kate couldn't exactly pinpoint.

Drifts of earthbound snow fluttered outside and Kate felt she could gaze through that kitchen window, enjoying the peace and the calm forever. Even dish washing was a chore she would gladly accept if this were the view and Deacon, her company.

"Any chance you're up for a late night walk?" Deacon dried his hands with a terrycloth dishtowel and then passed it to Kate, his hip pressed against the counter, legs crossed casually at the ankles. "Or are you ready to call it a night?"

"A walk would be lovely, Deacon." She folded the towel and slipped it back on the oven door handle, then hooked her thumb over her shoulder. "Just let me grab my coat real quick, okay?"

"Sure thing. Take your time."

Kate had returned to her barn loft that afternoon as the stairs were now repaired and it was finally safe to utilize them again. Even though that dedicated space was hers, she realized she'd much rather spend her time in the main farmhouse with Marla. Kate chalked it up to needing to make certain Marla didn't put any unnecessary strain on that wounded ankle, but in the end, Kate just didn't wish to be alone. She preferred company over isolation. And the company the Winters family offered was unmatched.

Deacon was waiting for her several paces from the house, his footprints leading a path through the otherwise untouched layer of powder. Before joining him, Kate paused to fully absorb the sight. Deacon's head was angled heavenward and the muted light from the crescent moon contoured the strong, distinct line of his jaw, making him as awe-inspiring as the creation surrounding him. His hands were shoved deeply into his tan, canvas coat pockets and if she stilled her breath and eliminated any other sound, Kate could make out the sweet, low hum of a well-known holiday song vibrating softly from his chest.

"*Walking in a Winter Wonderland*," she acknowledged quietly when she took her place next to him. "That's your favorite Christmas carol, isn't it?"

Swinging his gaze to look at her, Deacon's eyes sparked with joy. "You guessed it." He kicked up a clod of snow, toeing his boot against the icy edges. "When I was little, I thought the song was actually called *Walking in a Winters Wonderland.* I thought it was so cool that someone would write a carol just for us. My dad had to correct me many years later and disclose that it was *winter*, not Winters. But it never changed the connection I felt with the song. Still hasn't." His focus fastened on Kate and behind it was a palpable energy, his chestnut eyes never blinking when he parted his lips and half-sang, half-spoke the lines, "A beautiful sight…we're happy tonight…"

"Walking in a winter wonderland." Kate finished the chorus on a breath. Her mouth went dry and the need to swallow was strong as she observed the irrefutably handsome man at her shoulder. When his hand tugged from his pocket and his thumb and finger moved to tip her chin, beckoning her to turn closer to him, Kate suddenly felt her heart thudding in her ears as her pulse thrummed wildly with expectation. His other large hand gently lighted on her cheek, his thumb sweeping across her skin there, and when he stooped down and his mouth hovered mere inches from hers, Kate decided to meet him halfway. She lifted onto her tiptoes and pressed her lips to Deacon's in a long-awaited, tender kiss.

Shivers skittered up her spine and her body trembled with anticipation. Of course, she had kissed other men before, but standing with Deacon under the pale winter moonlight, his strong presence a protection against the cold and his heart a gift she almost didn't feel worthy to receive, she realized she'd never experience a connection like this again. Deacon was her perfect match. The marshmallow to her hot cocoa. The mittens to her scarf. The sturdy and proud evergreen to her yuletide season.

He was all of those things and her heart recognized the rarity in finding and falling so deeply for someone in such a short manner of time. *On the Job with Kate Carmichael* taught her a lot over the years, but the knowledge that a person like Deacon reciprocated her affection was the greatest discovery yet.

When he pulled back from their soft and slow kiss, his eyes met hers as the full weight of the moment settled upon them. Mouth tipping into a smile, he let out a small chuckle and before Kate knew it, she found herself doing the same, this part-nervous, part-elated giggle slipping between her lips while a warm blush crept over her cheeks.

"Wow." Deacon's fingers rubbed the back of his neck. "That was pretty great."

"That was the best first kiss I've ever had. I mean, it's not every day a girl gets kissed on a mountaintop in the falling snow surrounded by a magical forest of Christmas trees. It's the stuff of holiday fairytales."

"Or maybe we're just lucky enough that it's our reality." He slipped his hand between them and caught hers. "I ran into someone at the store today and they said the chance encounter was serendipitous. I didn't agree in that particular case, but maybe *this*"—he lifted their joined hands—"maybe this is serendipity, Kate. Destiny. Maybe the rough patch the tree farm went through— which ultimately prompted my mom to reach out to your station—was all part of this bigger picture we get to be a part of. I'm done pretending my past heartbreak didn't serve a purpose." He dropped her hand and took her delicately by the shoulders. "If I never learned the value of my heart and what it felt like in pieces, I'd never fully comprehend just how incredible it is to have it made whole again."

It wasn't often that Kate was rendered speechless. Somehow, Deacon's confession stole every word from her vocabulary, every thought from her mind. All she could do was express herself in the only way she knew how in the moment, and that was to tug the collar of his jacket, beckoning him closer as she swept her lips against his in another kiss that made her feelings known. A reciprocation of her hope, her admiration.

"I could get used to this," Deacon whispered against her mouth when they finally pulled back for breath. His eyes turned sorrowful when he said, "But I don't want to get used to the idea of you leaving in a week."

"Let's not think about that yet." She slipped her arms around his waist and drew him close, pressing her cheek against his chest, resting in the steady sound of his heartbeat echoing in her ear. "I'm here now. That's all that matters."

Kate couldn't pinpoint the exact moment their embrace shifted into something more, but suddenly they were moving side to side, dancing in a little circle as their boots crunched the icy snow underfoot. His hum from earlier gained volume as Deacon serenaded her with the purest renditions of holiday songs. They swayed to *Silent Night*. They twirled to *Here Comes Santa Claus*. They picked up their tempo when they sang *Joy to the World* and they laughed when Deacon chased the high notes and missed, his voice cracking as it strained out of range.

She would've willed the night to go on forever if she could. They racked their brains at the end of each song, pulling another carol from somewhere in the recesses of their holiday memories. Deacon even knew a few melodies Kate had never heard, and she let the new words of hope and love, peace and joy fill her spirit.

When she felt the vibration of her phone in her coat pocket, she did everything in her power to ignore it. What a change from that afternoon when she had stared at the blank screen gripped in her hands, begging the cellphone to light up with her boss's number.

"Do you need to get that?" Deacon stopped swaying and nudged his chin.

"It can wait."

He smiled. "Kate, you should really answer it. I know it's killing you not to. Go ahead. I don't mind. Really."

The thought of this night coming to an end was like the bittersweet letdown of unwrapping the very last Christmas present. Before the incoming call would be sent to voicemail, she retrieved her phone from her jacket and swiped the screen.

"Hello?"

"Well, there you are!" Courtney's nasally voice cut into the receiver. "Could you *be* a little harder to get ahold of?"

Well, yes. I could, Kate mused but kept the snide comment to herself. She stepped out from the circle of Deacon's arms. "Hi, Courtney. I'm glad we could finally connect. How are things at the station?"

"Listen, I don't have a lot of time, so I'm going to cut to the chase. I'm pulling you from the farm."

"You're what?" Kate plunged her finger into her ear in an effort to catch that sentence again. There was no way she'd heard it correctly.

"The farm piece is done."

Turning her back and stepping further out of earshot, away from Deacon who had busied himself with some impromptu stargazing, his eyes angling up toward the brilliant winter tapestry, Kate said in a hushed tone, "But I still have another week here. I'm only halfway done."

"Nope. Not anymore. It was cute and the social media thing was fine for that particular piece, but I've got a better lineup for you. Plus, we were able to hire a new cameraman more quickly than I anticipated, so I can move Toby back over to you. He'll be heading your way tomorrow. He's all yours again."

"Heading my way?" None of this made any sense. If Courtney truly wanted to put a premature end to the Yuletide Farm piece, Kate couldn't understand why Toby would be coming to the Sierras. She just assumed she'd be the one packing up and driving down to the Sacramento valley.

"He's going to meet you at the address I'm about to give you. Be there tomorrow at noon and not a minute later. Do you have something you can write it down on?"

"Hold on. I'll put you on speaker so I can type it into my phone." Kate noticed Deacon's eyes dart her direction as she juggled the phone and clicked the appropriate button. "Okay, go ahead."

"It's a chalet penthouse. The address is 5856 Ski Slope Lane in the North Lake area. You're going to be blown away when you find out who it is."

"No hints?" Kate asked, her curiosity getting the better of her, briefly eclipsing the sadness she felt at the thought of leaving Yuletide Farm.

"All I'm going to say is that this will be your most prestigious gig yet. No more measly tree farms for you. Get ready to take *On the Job with Kate Carmichael* to an entirely new level." Courtney laughed into the phone when she added, "Or I suppose I should say, an entirely new altitude."

DEACON

Deacon broke his own rule without even meaning to. That address tiptoed around his brain all night. By midnight, he had the street number typed into an internet search bar and a headshot of J.C. Patterson —women's downhill Olympic gold medalist—smiling brightly through the screen.

Smiling at him like she hadn't upended his future.

For the second time.

Jennifer Christine Patterson was nicknamed the impossible dreamer. That's what her father had labeled her early on and it stuck to her like glue. But Deacon never let Jenny believe there was any truth in that name. Mostly because he didn't believe it. If Jenny set her mind to something, it would happen. Nothing was impossible. And now it looked as though all of her dreams—the very ones that ultimately led to the demise of their relationship and severed their brief engagement —were finally coming true.

They'd met one December afternoon when Deacon had delivered a Christmas tree to her grandparents' mountain cabin a few miles up the road from the farm. She'd just returned from Colorado to stay for the winter while she searched for a new trainer. An avid skier that dominated as a high school athlete, a college student with a full-ride, and then—at the time of their introduction—an Olympic hopeful with a promising future and unbeatable personal best, Jenny became the town darling. Everyone loved her. Including Deacon.

He loved her so much that he strapped two slick, thin boards to his feet and catapulted down a perfectly good mountain at breakneck speed, just to have the opportunity to be by her side. He was an abominable skier, bailing more often than not, but skiing was Jenny's passion and purpose and Deacon reveled in the chance to be a part of that, even if it meant risking life and limb on a daily basis just so he could remain in her sphere.

Jenny's enthusiasm was contagious, her zeal infectious. At that point in Deacon's life, he not only needed that, but required it to go on. Like a salve to his grief, their relationship helped Deacon place one foot in front of the other after his father's death. Maybe it was more like one ski in front of the other, but either way, the forward motion was good and necessary.

Until the day she unveiled her biggest dream yet. In recent times, when Deacon would think back on this fateful moment, he'd often wonder if his kneejerk reaction had been the right one. But then all it took was saddling Bella to ride up and down the acres of their generational farm to confirm his decision was, in fact, the only one he could make.

"Can't you see it?" Jenny had said on a starless Christmas Eve night, her hand fanning over the tree-tipped valley below in an all-encompassing sweep. She had tugged on Deacon's hand excitedly from their perch on a bench at the apex of the mountain. *"I mean, it's a little hard now, what with all the evergreens, but once those are cleared out, you'll be able to envision it completely. It'll be perfect."*

The day his grandfather died—just two short years after Deacon's own father's passing—Deacon became a first-time land owner, to the tune of a fifteen-hundred-acre Christmas tree farm. He had never bothered to calculate the property's monetary value because no amount of printed paper would ever cover its worth. It was as priceless as the lives of the men who farmed the land before him.

When Deacon looked out over the acreage, he saw each individual tree, every growth ring in every trunk, every needle-covered branch meant for boasting strands of twinkle lights and heirloom ornaments.

Jenny saw dollar signs.

A ski resort, more specifically, run by a future Olympic hopeful. *"It's like this mountain was created to be skied on,"* she'd say, each conversation another effort to twist Deacon's arm. *"The double black diamond will go where that old tree is. You know, the giant one with the plaque that says something about a bunch of needles. That terrain is made for it."*

Try as he might, Deacon couldn't create that scene, even in his imagination. Every weekend, Jenny would take him to the local slopes to test out a myriad of trails, as though all it would take was the perfect run down the mountain to suddenly be onboard. Deacon just couldn't get there.

And when he crashed like he figured he inevitably would, injuring himself sufficiently to be laid up in the hospital during the farm's busiest season, he knew enough to recognize his own future crashing down around him, too.

Jenny didn't even press pause on her plans to transform the tree farm into the ski resort of her biggest and boldest dreams. The day she came to visit him at the hospital, cardboard tube of professional drawings in hand along with a note from a potential investor and a naïve, hope-filled smile on her face, Deacon did the only thing left to do. He ended their whirlwind engagement, wished her well, and closed the door on a life where someone else called the shots on his forever.

He'd stuck to his vow and hadn't looked her up until that night. He'd heard gossip around town as to her whereabouts, but he never truly kept tabs on her. That was his rule. Maybe he should have. Then he would have known that two years ago, she'd married mogul Bryce McCullough, a CEO from Park City and heir to his family's brand of luxury ski chalets. It appeared Jenny had finally found someone to share the very specific vision for her future, and while Deacon felt a sliver of happiness over that outcome, he also felt cheated on the deepest level when it came to love.

And now Kate was set to leave and his heart felt cheated all over again.

"You have to tell her." Marla flipped the serving spoon over and a clump of scrambled eggs plopped onto Deacon's plate, right next to the links of maple sausage and dry piece of toast that spent a minute too long in the toaster slot. "She has to know, Deacon. It's only fair."

He drank his coffee slowly and then lowered the mug to the table, spinning the handle around mindlessly as he shrugged. "What good will it do? You and I both know Kate. Out of conviction alone, she'll put an end to it. This is a huge opportunity for her. Jenny is a big name and her husband is even bigger. I'm not going to jeopardize that."

Marla sighed. "I know. You're right. But none of this *feels* right. What Jenny did to you—"

"Jenny didn't do anything to me, Mom. We just weren't on the same page when it came to our futures."

"Don't get me wrong, I liked her, I did. You can't help but like Jenny. But the way she tried to diminish what this property means to you…What it means to our family…" Marla's chin quivered. She shoved the back of her hand to her eyes and halted whatever impending emotion threatened to spill. "Well—I'm just not sure I'll ever be over that."

Deacon touched his mother's arm. Marla forced a smile, making her sadness take a backseat. "Can I top off your coffee for you?" She reached for Deacon's half-full mug.

"I'm good." He didn't need any more of the bitter

drink churning and irritating his stomach. It already ached enough each time his thoughts circled back to Kate and her impending departure. When he'd over-heard she'd be staying in the Sierras for her next assign-ment, he couldn't help but settle into relief. They'd have more time together. They would need to work around their schedules and fit things in where they could, but she wouldn't be gone forever.

He wasn't so sure that would be the case now.

"Good morning!" Kate's singsong greeting put Deacon's head on swivel. She strolled into the dining room, her face as radiant as the morning sun that passed through the downstairs windows and backlit her in rich streams of honey-yellow light.

"Morning, Kate." Marla had recovered from her earlier falter in composure, no current sign of sorrow on her face. She slid out a chair for Kate and began making up a breakfast plate. "Take a seat. I've got a new pot of coffee percolating now. Should be ready in just a few."

"Thank you, Marla. This smells wonderful. But should you be on—?"

"It's a wasted effort," Deacon interjected. "Believe me, I've tried."

Marla's brow pinched and she gave a little frown of defiance. "I've stayed off this ankle for as long as I'm able to. You get to be my age and if you go too long without using something, it'll quit on you altogether."

"Like your hearing?" Deacon teased. "Is that the issue?"

"I can hear you just fine, son. I'm just not *listening* to you."

Kate chuckled. She picked up her fork and plunged it into the fluffy, golden eggs, then suspended the bite in front of her mouth. "If I don't finish my plate, it has nothing to do with your cooking. My stomach is a million butterflies right now. Not sure there's any space for food."

"You nervous about today?" Deacon lifted his mug.

"Deacon." She lowered the loaded fork to her plate and leaned over the table, her voice dipping to a whisper. "I looked that address up. Do you know who it belongs to?"

The question was rhetorical and he didn't want to lie, so he let the silence prompt Kate to continue.

"J.C. Patterson." Kate's volume dialed up several decibels. "The Olympic gold medalist. Deacon, I'm going to learn how to downhill ski from one of the best athletes of our generation." There was both awe and fear bound up in her words. "This is big. Really big."

"It sounds like an incredible opportunity." He exchanged a brief look with his mother before Marla hobbled into the kitchen to check on the brewing coffee.

"I'm going to see if I can bring you by for an introduction."

"Kate, you don't have to—"

"I mean, it might take a few days before I have the opportunity to ask, but I'm thinking your farm would be perfect to supply trees for their ski resort chalets. If you could get an account with the McCulloughs—I mean, gosh, can you even imagine? That would be really incredible, right?"

Kate's heart was in the right place—the perfect

place, even—but Deacon couldn't offer more than a smile that he hoped didn't come across as disingenuous as it felt.

"Just focus on this opportunity for you, Kate. It's a great one. Don't worry about me."

She raised the fork back up and popped the scrambled eggs into her mouth. "Oh, wow. These are really good." Turning in her chair, she called out over her shoulder, "Marla, you've outdone yourself this time! The eggs are amazing!"

Deacon watched Kate while she consumed her breakfast, noting how every part of life—even down to mealtime—was an experience for her. There was no denying the similarities between Kate and Jenny. They were both exuberant, over-the-top in their emotions. But where Jenny's drive and passion focused narrowly on herself and the goals she hoped to personally achieve, Kate was the most inclusive person Deacon had ever encountered. She was driven by the success of others, and her thoughts were, more often than not, outwardly focused.

Kate was the sort of person that challenged you to become a better one yourself. For that very reason, Deacon buttoned his lip throughout the rest of their breakfast and let her bask in the anticipation of this upcoming opportunity, because it truly was a good one. Yes, Jenny had once ruined things for Deacon, but if that's what needed to happen to get to this moment, he'd gladly go through it all again.

Deacon would suffer heartbreak a hundred times

over if it meant Kate had even one shot at the success she so deserved.

KATE

The chaste kiss Deacon lowered to her lips right before Kate rolled up her driver's side window felt more like an ellipsis than a period. It wasn't a goodbye; it was an until later. This new arrangement was the best of both worlds, really. When Courtney said Kate's stint at the farm was over, she didn't want to think what that might mean for her budding new relationship with Deacon. That she would be a mere fifteen-minute drive up the highway was—as Deacon might put it —serendipitous.

She didn't know how Courtney was able to arrange such a prestigious lineup, but Kate didn't question it. J.C. Patterson was the world's best when it came to downhill skiing, and her fame—both locally and nationally—would do wonders for the show. Not that any of that had ever been all that important to Kate, but the added exposure this might bring was exciting, nevertheless.

The drive was quick and she glimpsed the impressive mountain chalet before her GPS instructed her to take the next exit. The alpine building peeked through the trees like a woodland castle in a fairytale setting. As her sedan hugged the curve of the road, the building crept closer into sight until the enormity of the chalet took up her entire windshield view. There stood one main structure—front and center—with attached wings, alike in appearance but smaller in scale. A wide rooftop reminiscent of Swiss architecture sloped out over the thick, wooden exterior and the overlay of snow that clung to the ridge of the chalet looked like it belonged there year round.

The sight was stunning in an almost overwhelming way. Kate followed the bend up to the building's entrance, not at all surprised when a man in a valet uniform stepped up to her car after she rolled to a stop. This was just the sort of place that would afford its guests those certain luxuries. She gathered her bags from her trunk, handed over her keys, and followed the bellhop through the expansive doors that parted for her like she was a starlet taking a stroll on the red carpet.

"Right this way." He bent an arm and guided her inside.

If a smell could be expensive, the aroma of the lobby was easily worth a year of her salary, maybe more. Kate inhaled deeply, pondering how she might be able to bottle up that scent and take it home with her. It was so opulent she nearly lost her breath.

"Miss Carmichael?" A young woman in a pencil skirt, black fitted blazer, and cat eye glasses sauntered up with her hand extended, readying for a shake. "I'm glad to see you've made it safely. I'm Tammy Porch, Ms. Patterson's assistant. Your cameraman, Toby, is already here. Can I show you up? The bellman will see to it that your belongings are delivered to your room."

"Oh, thank you," Kate answered. Her eyes continued their slow perusal of the chalet lobby as she trailed Tammy to the elevator. A tree fit for Times Square was erected in the very center of the massive room with heavy glass ornaments and red beaded garland that coiled up its tapered branches in big, swaggy loops. Vintage wooden skis were positioned and balanced between the branches and poles stuck out in such a unique way that it had to be the work of a professional decorator. The creativity was off the charts.

"That tree is phenomenal," Kate gaped.

"Isn't it?" Tammy punched the button to the elevator and when the doors spread wide apart, she indicated for Kate to step inside first. "The McCulloughs recently acquired an artificial tree company." The doors slid closed, leaving the two women alone in the small, box-like space. Tammy waved a fob over a button on the wall and the elevator lurched into motion. "It's quite genius, really. You go online, pick the variety and size tree you'd like and it shows up on your doorstep three days later, along with a box of decorations. There are all kinds of themes to choose from. One for every budget. This particular display—as you could probably guess— is called *Mountain Ski Chalet*."

That information would have held Kate's interest,

maybe even piqued it, had she not already concocted a plan to suggest a partnership with Deacon's farm. The hope of a symbiotic relationship forming was squashed before she even had a chance to meet the infamous J.C.

"I haven't seen your show before." Tammy stated it so matter-of-factly that it didn't come across as an insult, so Kate didn't take it that way.

"I haven't met your boss before," Kate countered with a shrug and a smile.

"Oh, you'll love her. Everyone does." She paused a second, almost weighing whether or not to add the next part. "Bryce, though. He's not exactly…warm."

"Well, his family does own a plethora of ski resorts. Maybe that has a little something to do with it." Kate almost rolled her own eyes at her stupid joke. Luckily, the elevator doors yawned open before she could continue in her pathetic, nervous comedic routine.

Tammy stepped out. "Wait here a moment while I see if they're ready for you."

The best view Kate had encountered in ages greeted her, and it wasn't the majestic, snowcapped mountain range standing in the distance on the other side of the penthouse's wall-to-wall windows.

"Toby!" Kate sprinted into her dear friend's arms.

Her cameraman scooped her into a giant hug that lifted her feet from the ground. "*Reunited and it feels so good*," Toby sang into her hair in such a silly voice it had Kate erupting with laughter. A familiar face was exactly what she needed. While the chalet was spectacular, there was nothing cozy or even comfortable about it. But

Toby was comfort. Always had been, always would be. "If Courtney ever makes me work with Carl Weathers again, I just might give her my two-week notice."

"That bad?"

"You know he wears a toupee, right? Well, the man keeps it in a box, Kate. A box."

Kate played the devil's advocate. "Remember that one time I got extensions? Those weren't cheap. I can sort of see why he'd do that."

"But he *named* it. The toupee. He named the toupee Harry."

"Okay." Kate snorted. "That is a little weird."

"Did you know he takes it on and off between filming?" Toby's expression was incredulous. "And guess who gets to hold that box? Yep, yours truly. *'Would you mind taking care of Harry while I go grab a bite to eat? Thanks, Tobs. You're the best.'* " Toby shuddered. "Never again. Never again."

Kate had heard rumors of Carl and his oddities. She counted herself lucky that she hadn't been partnered with him on assignments as of yet. "I promise I won't make you hold my hair. Only that one time when I got that horrible bout of food poisoning after the oyster shucking piece we did. Man, that was awful. I still can't really do seafood."

"I'd gladly hold your hair any day, Kate. And I'll put it out there while I'm at it: I'll also accompany you to lavish ski resorts any time you need me to." His eyes popped open wide. "Is this place unreal or what?"

"Unreal. That is definitely the right word for it."

As their conversation closed, Tammy reappeared, beckoning the duo. "Everyone's ready. Right this way."

She led them down a long marble corridor to a study that shared the same mountainscape view as the grand entry. An attractive couple sat in twin tufted, plaid chairs, a crackling fire in a white rock hearth at their back and a bearskin rug—complete with head still intact—at their feet. The man wore a cream turtleneck sweater with a detailed argyle pattern spread across the collar that put all of Kate's knitted creations to shame. An air of pretension clung to his every feature, all the way down to his leather loafers that likely cost more than Kate's down payment on her home.

Oddly, the woman was less intimidating. No doubt the outfit adorning her slim figure was every bit as expensive as her husband's, but she had a friendly twinkle in her eyes that sparked even brighter when she stood from her seat to meet her guests halfway.

"I'm so happy to finally meet you," J.C. said, words Kate had readied on her own tongue to deliver. "I'm glad everything worked out for you to be here." She enveloped Kate in a hug, and once she released her, did the same with Toby. "Have a seat, please. Can we get you anything to drink? Coffee? Wine?"

"Oh, I'm fine. Thank you."

"I believe we're all out of wine, dear," the man spoke up. His hands were folded in his lap and he looked like he had no plans to entertain his company. Definitely not serve them beverages.

"I grabbed some from the store the other day. Three bottles."

His neutral expression turned firm. "We have people to do that for us, Jennifer. You don't have to go into town. Certainly not to buy your own alcohol."

J.C. rolled her eyes and turned back to Kate. "Let's just say Bryce and I grew up a little differently. I'm still not quite used to letting people do things I'm fully capable of doing on my own."

"So it's Jennifer," Kate asked, circling back to Bryce's statement. She'd been curious what the J.C. stood for.

"Yes, Jennifer Christine, but those closest to me used to call me Jenny. I switched to J.C. right before the Olympics. I had just gone through a rough patch—made some really big personal changes—and I figured a name change might be fitting, too. Clean slate sort of thing and all."

"I get that," Kate said.

"Anyway, like I said, we're so glad you're here. I think we're going to have a lot of fun with this." Kate fluffed up a fur trimmed pillow on the couch near their chairs and patted her hand on the cushion. "Please, have a seat."

Toby and Kate plopped down in unison, the leather hissing as their weight settled on the plush sofa.

"How does this whole thing work?" J.C. took her place at her husband's side.

"*On the Job*? Well, it's honestly just as it sounds. I'll follow you around for a predetermined amount of time and you'll show me the ins and outs of what it's like to be a competitive downhill skier. Toby will film it all and at the end, we'll go back into the studio to edit before it's ready for production," Kate explained. "I have to be upfront with you, though. I don't have a lot of recent skiing experience. It's been a few years since I've been on the slopes."

When J.C. and Bryce exchanged private glances, Kate felt a knot form in the pit of her stomach, like maybe she misspoke without even realizing it.

Bryce cleared his throat for no other reason than to break the stilted silence that ensued. "I think there's been a bit of a misunderstanding."

"Oh?" Panic seized Kate's throat which made it suddenly difficult to swallow. "There has?"

"It isn't Jennifer's job we'd like you to shadow, it's mine. Rather, *ours*, I suppose."

Kate could roll with that. She recently had ample practice in doing that very thing. "I see. That shouldn't be a problem at all. I've job shadowed just about everything out there. I can be flexible."

"Good, good." Bryce nodded and appraised her with a steady, concentrated gaze. "As you likely already know, my family is in the ski resort business. Acquiring land. Purchasing existing lodges and turning them around with the use of our powerful brand and our tried and true marketing strategies. We're right in the middle of this particular mountainside venture and aren't even set to open until next calendar year, yet we've presold every chalet and have a waiting list for future builds. So I currently have my eyes on another possible land acquisition. One that's just a few miles down the road." His steel-gray eyes slivered and his fingers steepled in front of his mouth when he said, "You might have heard of it, actually. Right now it's just a bunch of trees, but give us a year and it'll be the hottest resort to hit the Sierras. That's a McCullough guarantee."

DEACON

Deacon hadn't seen Kate in four days. He realized that wasn't very long, but considering they'd only spent one week together, by comparison, it felt like an eternity. She had texted that first night. Nothing long, just a few lines saying she missed him and that she would call in the morning.

That call never happened and when lunchtime rolled around and his phone buzzed with a text that read: *Sorry. Got caught up with a few things. Will touch base tonight*, it was as though he could feel his heart dropping into the depths of his stomach, like an anchor thrown overboard wrenching it downward.

Something wasn't right, but he didn't know Kate well enough to discern just what that might be. This was the hard truth he couldn't evict from his thoughts.

Maybe in his absence she'd come to her senses. Their lives were different. He thought back to the first day when she had set foot on the farm, all high heels and a confidence he assumed was misplaced. How wrong he had been. Kate had unfurled during her time at Yuletide. He saw her transform from someone who had a job to do, into a person who belonged there, like she had officially joined their team.

The thought of Kate on another team—on Jenny's, no less—made him wince. But that's what had happened. The fact that she couldn't break away long enough for a brief quick call only reiterated the fact that Kate had thrown herself completely into this new assignment. Deacon had a hard time being frustrated with that. When it all boiled down, that's exactly what Kate needed to do. What she *should* do.

The farm once again became Deacon's primary focus. Without the steady online publicity Kate's show provided, numbers dwindled by the day. Their fifteen minutes of fame were up. He wasn't surprised. He knew the influx of visitors was largely due to Kate's influence. From that moment, he made it a practice to fully appreciate every packed car that rolled into their lot and every tree that left strapped to its rooftop. He valued his customers more than ever before, and each day closer to Christmas he grew in gratitude. For the farm. For his family. For his time with Kate, however brief.

When two weeks hit and their communication ceased altogether, Deacon did everything he could to keep from feeling the pain that had once been so familiar it was like a life sentence. He let her go. He had to. And he wasn't going to wallow. He would find joy, even in the middle of this because joy wasn't tied to circumstance. He knew that. Joy was all around and when you couldn't see or feel it, sometimes you had to manufacture it.

One night, after shutting down the farm with the help of Cody and his mother, Deacon saddled up Bella and rode down the mountain, the stars above the only guiding light as he and his horse wove in and out of stalks of evergreen. The low hoot of an owl marked out time like a second hand on an old clock. A brisk wind swirled through the trees. Deacon flipped up the collar on his jacket and shuddered against the weather. He didn't know what he was looking for—or even that he was looking for something in particular—until his eyes fastened on it.

Kate's tree. The one she had all but destroyed during their pruning session.

Deacon's heart squeezed.

"Whoa there, girl," he murmured to Bella as he pulled up on her reins, easing her into a gradual stop. Slinging his leg over, he lowered from the horse, then gathered the rope he kept tied to the saddle horn and bound up the tree. Like a pack mule, Bella didn't falter when Deacon hoisted the prickly object onto her back. He returned to his saddle and guided her up the summit, hope now a beacon like the North star that had guided him there.

IT WAS DIFFICULT TO DECORATE A TREE THAT HAD SIX-inch branches, but Deacon made it work. If anything, he told himself it displayed the ornaments all the better.

They couldn't get lost in dense needles or overshadowed by other decorations that shared the same branch. One ornament fit on one branch and that was it. By eight o'clock, Deacon had decked every available portion of the tree with keepsake ornaments from a box he had stored in his hall closet so long the layer of dust was as thick as the lid. He sat in his recliner with a mug of hot chocolate (a recipe he stole from one of Kate's viewers), his heart harkening back to the memories each ornament embodied.

He wondered why he'd gone so long without his own tree. Maybe it was a cobbler's child with no shoes sort of thing. Still, he pledged never to go another Christmas without one.

When he'd emptied his mug, he raised from his chair, pondering if he should heat up another cup or ultimately call it a night.

"What do you think, Rascal?" The dog perked up, roused from his nearby nap. "Should we head to bed?"

Rascal barked.

"Is that a yes?" Deacon prodded. He needed some clarification. "Or a no."

The Labrador howled again.

"How about this: two barks for yes, one bark for no."

Rascal suddenly bounded past, narrowly knocking Deacon to the ground in an all out race down the hall. "Settle down, boy."

Following on the canine's heels, Deacon crossed the house to the front door where Rascal twirled impatiently in a spinning motion that made him look like he was chasing his tail.

"Settle down," Deacon instructed again. "What do you think is out there, boy? A squirrel? Santa's reindeer?" He pulled on the door handle to investigate the root of all the commotion.

"Not a reindeer." Kate lifted her hand in a timid wave. "Sorry if that's a disappointment. I can see if I can round some up real quick, if you like."

Deacon's jaw unhinged. "Kate. I… I wasn't expecting you."

She shivered, then ran her palms along her arms and shifted side to side, both her gaze and her body.

"Come in." He waved her inside. "Come on in out of that snow."

She hesitated, then accepted the invitation but the tension was there. He felt it and he knew she could, too. It hung between them like a breath in the cold.

"Can I take your coat?" He already had his hands out for it.

She slipped it off and passed her navy wool jacket to him. "Thank you, Deacon."

He examined her face a moment but he couldn't read it, no matter how hard he tried.

"I'm sorry to just show up like this."

"It's okay. Really." He chanced a look into the interior of his home, wondering if Kate would be more comfortable by the radiating warmth of the fire or if she would rather say what she came to say right here in the foyer. Just get it over with.

"Can we talk?"

"Of course." His hope rose at the promise of her words. "Is the family room okay?"

"Yes. That would be great." She followed behind with her hands clasped in front of her. He knew the exact moment she caught sight of the tree. The little breath that escaped her lips gave it away. "Deacon. You put up a tree."

"Not just any tree." He rushed over and gestured from top to bottom in his best game show host impression. "This is a Kate Carmichael special."

Her hand flew to her mouth to squelch a small laugh. "Oh gosh. Please tell me it's not."

"It really is. You know, I think you might be onto something with this particular pruning job. It really showcases the individual ornaments so effectively. I think this could totally catch on."

Kate's gaze softened as she smiled wistfully, but Deacon picked up the hesitation in her reaction.

"Can I get you anything? You hungry? Thirsty?"

"No. Thank you, though." She slowly lowered to the couch, then bound up her hands in her lap again. Her gaze roamed about the room before coming back to Deacon and remaining there. "Deacon, I owe you an apology."

He took a seat directly beside her, wanting to be close but unsure if that was okay. "Kate—"

"I've been thinking about how to say all of this, so I'm just going to say it." Her eyes shut, then popped back open. "I'm sorry I left you for something more exciting."

He hadn't thought of their situation in those precise words, but he supposed that's exactly what had occurred. That stung just a bit. "It's really okay, Kate—"

"No." She shook her head tightly. "It's not. I never should have taken that job with Jenny and Bryce. I should've pushed to finish out *this* job. I should've been committed to what I promised your mother when we arranged everything back at the beginning."

"You don't have to worry about us, Kate. We're fine."

"But I do. I do worry because I know I've hurt you, and I hate that it's in the same way you've been hurt before."

He didn't quite follow. "What do you mean?"

"I left because I thought maybe there was a bigger story for me. I got caught up in the excitement of that. I had no idea that's exactly what Jenny did to you."

"You and Jenny are not the same at all, Kate. Don't for one minute compare this situation to what happened between me and her."

"But there are comparisons. Painful ones. I had no clue she wanted to clear cut the farm and turn it into a resort, Deacon. I honestly didn't even know that you knew her."

He reached out to still her hands. They were wringing together incessantly. "Because I didn't tell you. I didn't want to stand in the way of this opportunity for you, Kate."

"I wish you would have." A sheen filled her gaze as her eyes slid down to her lap, regarding Deacon's hands that encased and steadied her own. "I've already put in my two weeks."

"On the job?" He was surprised to hear that things had wrapped up so quickly, but couldn't say he wasn't relieved.

"No. I put in my two weeks at the station."

"Kate." Deacon's expression fell blank. "Why would—?"

"That's where I've been this whole time. Back in Sacramento sorting things out and buttoning everything up. I didn't want to come back here until all of that was put to bed and finished," she explained. "I didn't even last a day at Bryce and Jenny's. When he told me his ultimate goal was to convince you to sell, I realized I couldn't be a part of something like that. Not even if it made for good T.V." She leaned closer to punctuate the words. "And then when I found out that was why things had ended with Jenny—that she pushed and pushed for you to give up your dream for hers—I packed up my car and didn't stop driving until I was at Courtney's front door with my resignation letter."

"You didn't have to do any of that, Kate. You didn't have to quit. We could've figured something out."

"But I did have to," she insisted. "I've always said that *On the Job* has been like holding a hundred different job interviews, but that *I'm* the one conducting them. Well, I've finally made my decision." She took a fortifying breath and stared straight into Deacon's eyes, her gaze the most intense shade of blue he'd ever seen. "Deacon Winters, I'd officially like to be a part of your permanent staff here at Yuletide Tree Farm. If you're hiring."

"You want to be a Christmas tree farmer?" A sound

of disbelief left his mouth. "Out of all the jobs you are qualified for?"

"I want to be a wreath maker and a tree hauler and a pie burner and a terrible snowmobile driver. Whatever you need me for, I'll be it. I'm in. One-hundred-percent. I can rent out the loft and I promise to work harder than I ever have on any job. I'll be your best employee."

"What if I just want you to be Kate."

Her eyes clouded and her head twitched slightly in confusion.

"I just want you, Kate," he said again. "No expectations. No titles. Honestly, these last two weeks have been rough; I'm not going to lie. Not knowing where we stood or what the future held kept me up at night. More than usual, which is saying a lot. I just want you in my life, Kate. This Christmas and as many Christmases as you're willing to stick around."

Moving closer, Kate slipped under Deacon's arm and lowered her head to his shoulder, cocooning into his side like she was made to be there. Deacon prayed she felt at home there, like the way his heart felt now that it fully belonged to hers. Together they gazed past the laughable little tree and out toward the vast array of evergreens that brought them together in the best twist of fate Deacon could ever hope for.

"I plan to stick around for a long time, Deacon Winters," Kate said. She snuggled closer and added, "A very long time. That's one job I can definitely tackle."

"Looks like getting hitched went off without a hitch." Cody clanked the neck of his bottle to Deacon's in an informal toast and then tossed back a swallow. "Can you believe it? Husband and wife. Didn't think I'd live to see the day."

"After two years of waiting to marry the woman of my dreams, you know, I actually *can* believe it." Deacon's eyes tracked Kate across the church fellowship hall. She'd had the same entourage of eager little girls following her all evening, as though she were their favorite princess and they wanted nothing more than to bask in her magical presence. Deacon could understand why. Kate was nothing short of enchanting. In her off-the-shoulder, lace gown with beaded bodice that fishtailed into a swirl of pristine, white fabric at her feet, she looked every bit a royal.

When the church doors spread that afternoon, silhouetting his bride in the most ethereal winter sun they'd been blessed with all season, Deacon had to tug his bottom lip between his teeth to harness its tremble as thankful tears sloped over his cheeks. He was torn between wanting Kate to run down the aisle to get to him and wishing he could slow it all to fully savor each beautiful step she took toward their awaiting future.

With Toby by Kate's side and Cody by Deacon's, they pledged their lives, their love, and their hope to one another in a ceremony that had the whole town on their feet in cheers of heartfelt applause and ovation. It was the best day of Deacon's life, and yet, he knew this was only the beginning of many more just like it.

"Excuse me while I attempt to steal my bride away from that gaggle of girls over there." Deacon squeezed his brother's shoulder. "I'm not sure I'll be successful, though. I'm a bit outnumbered."

"Good luck. You'll need it," Cody said on a laugh. "I'll circle back with you in a bit."

"Sounds good, brother."

Deacon negotiated his way through the guests, stopping momentarily to accept well wishes and words of congratulation. He locked eyes with Kate just as Dottie Mason hauled him into a bear hug and a conversation about Pastor Tomlin's rambling Sunday sermon on extending grace to your fellow neighbor.

"I just think he should've included something about justice don't you? It can't be all grace and no justice. Maybe he's got that planned for next week," she babbled, unfazed by Deacon's determined beeline toward his new bride. "I just don't want the folks around here thinking we can go out giving away grace, willy-nilly. Mark Huxley accidentally cut down two trees that were technically on our property and did I give him grace for that? Sure, I did. But the justice side of things says he owes me two trees. I think he needs to pay up."

"You know, I think I could easily arrange for a couple of trees for you, Dottie." Deacon smiled. "Why don't you track Cody down and he can work out the details."

"Really? That would be incredible, Deacon. Now, I don't want to take up any more of your time, but there's an elder board meeting—"

"Mind if I steal this handsome fella for a moment?" Kate tapped Dottie on the shoulder and gave Deacon a wink.

"Oh, certainly," Dottie said. She stepped out from between the newly married couple. "I'll leave you two lovebirds alone. Enjoy your special day, sweeties. It was a beautiful ceremony. Just beautiful."

Deacon moved close to Kate. He dipped his hand to the curve of her waist and pulled her body flush to his. "I was just on my way to rescue you," he whispered into her hair that hung in loose curls at her shoulders.

"Then you would actually be the prince charming my little friends keep calling you." Kate placed her hands on Deacon's shoulders, then slid them to the back of his neck to draw him into a kiss. "I have to say…" She pulled back and met his gaze. "Everything about today has been nothing short of perfection, Deacon."

"That's all you." He looked around the room at the crowd, the decorations, the atmosphere in general that had every element of holiday splendor.

"To my credit, I've had some experience as a wedding planner. And a florist. And a baker, too, but I think it was a wise decision to hire out for the cake."

"I'm sure you could have done it," Deacon countered.

"Probably, but how awful would I feel if I gave all of our guests food poisoning? Some things are better left to the professionals."

"Maybe." Deacon shrugged. "But everything else was wedding perfection."

It had been Kate's idea to decorate the reception hall with cut trees and fresh wreaths from Deacon's farm, transforming the otherwise plain space into what she labeled the *Winters Wonderland*. And rather than requesting gifts from a registry, the couple had asked their family and friends to purchase and wrap a present to donate to the town's toy drive. Gratitude overtook him when Deacon noticed the mounds of gifts, all piled beneath their Yuletide trees. Even on a day Kate had every right to claim as her own, she thought of others. It looked like Christmas morning twenty times over and when he envisioned the faces of the children on the receiving end of that generosity, a ball of emotion tightened Deacon's throat. Kindness had a ripple effect and their wedding day was the start of that. To Deacon, that was the richest blessing of all.

The night was a joy-filled blur of toasts and dancing, fellowship and laughter. Just after nine, Cody summoned Deacon with a whistle, two fingers pressed between his lips to create the shrill sound. "Brother." He waved him near and dropped a set of keys into Deacon's palm. "I think it's about time we gave you and your bride a proper send off. Your truck is right out front."

Guests lined the walkway holding glittering sparklers that popped and snapped, showering the couple in shards of light like the flash of a thousand cameras. Deacon rushed Kate toward his beloved truck parked at the bottom of the staircase and he smiled when he noticed a wreath fastened to the bumper with a *Just Married* sign hung in the center.

He rounded the vehicle and held open the door for Kate while she bent to gather the fabric of her skirt and hoist herself into the truck. Deacon leaned forward, hands hooked on the roof and couldn't mask his smirk when he asked, "Ready to start our life together, Mrs. Winters?"

"I'D LIKE TO STOP BY THE BARN TO CHECK ON THE horses before we head to the cottage for the night. If that's okay."

"Sounds good to me." Kate smiled. She couldn't keep her eyes off her ring finger. Even now as they rode back to the farm, she stretched out her left arm and wriggled her hand, admiring the way the solitaire diamond caught and reflected light across the cab of Deacon's truck in rainbow prisms like a twirling disco ball. The stone was a modest size, nothing too showy or ornate, which fit Kate's tastes to a T.

"How are you liking your something new?" Deacon beamed, pride weighty in his look of shear devotion.

"I adore it, Deacon. It's so lovely. I can't stop staring at it." He caught her hand and brought it to his lips to press a kiss to her skin before releasing it and taking hold of the wheel with both hands again. "Did you happen to bring your something borrowed with you?"

Kate lifted the stunning fur stole from the seat and slipped it onto her bare shoulders. The shawl had belonged to Grandma Kay, then to Marla, and was now Kate's to pass down to future Winters women. She couldn't believe how impeccably it complimented her wedding dress, serving its purpose to create both warmth and beauty like it was always meant to be worn by her.

"Good." Deacon nodded again. "And your something old?"

Kate clicked her heels. The leather boots were only two years old, but she'd passed the hundred-hour break-in mark long ago and the scuff marks and scratches told the story of trail rides and tree farming as effectively as a memory. "Yep. Right here."

"So the only thing you didn't have is something blue, right?"

Shrugging, Kate affirmed Deacon's question with a little nod. The tradition hadn't been all that important to her, really, so she didn't spend too much time worrying about completing it. Blue didn't go with her holiday colors of deep, crimson reds and rich, earthy greens, so she opted to keep it out of the scheme altogether.

"I think I might be able to fix that." Deacon shifted into park several paces away from the barn, and when

Kate saw Bella tied to the hitching rail, she turned toward her new husband.

"What's Bella doing out at this hour?"

"That's our ride."

Kate punctuated her confusion with a quirk of her brow. "Our ride?"

"Yep." Deacon didn't add to that and when they exited the truck and came up by the horse's side, he let out a little snicker of remembrance.

"I know exactly what you're thinking," Kate said.

"Oh, do you?" Deacon linked his fingers together and lowered his hands to create a makeshift step to help Kate onto the bareback horse.

"When you saw me trying and failing to get into the saddle that day, did you ever think I would one day be your wife?"

"You know, there are very few instances in life where I'll gladly admit my misgivings. That one takes the cake. I've never been more grateful to have been so wrong about something. *So* very wrong."

Kate sat in a sidesaddle position, her gown billowing along the horse's flank in a sweeping display of ivory satin and lace. Deacon untied Bella from the rail, collected her reins and then joined his bride. Forget a horse drawn carriage, riding in the mountain snow atop Deacon's favorite horse was as romantic as it could get. Kate leaned up against Deacon's firm chest, allowing the rocking of Bella's steady, rhythmic gait to move their body's like a dance.

"Where are we headed?" Kate angled her head which gave Deacon a chance to steal a quick kiss.

"Only a bit further."

After a few minutes, Kate could sense the horse relax her pace, but she still couldn't determine their destination. When they came to a halt in the empty portion of the farm where the rental trees were stored in the off season, Kate's mounting interest turned into full-fledged curiosity.

"What are we doing out here, Deacon?" She took his hand as he helped her to the ground.

"We're here for your something blue."

Kate turned her eyes in every direction but still couldn't put two and two together. "I don't think I understand—"

Bending down, Deacon reached for a tray of saplings that rested on an old stump nearby. He held out the little, baby trees and grinned. "*Blue* spruce."

"Oh goodness, Deacon. They are adorable." She ran her hands over the prickly surface full of silver-tipped needles.

Deacon pulled a single sapling from its container and while it wasn't more than a few inches tall, Kate could already see the little coil of stringy roots tangling and twisting as they established themselves in the clod of dirt.

"I want to watch these trees grow and flourish over the years, just like our love." He wrapped Kate's hands around the miniature tree and then cupped his own over them, cradling the evergreen in their palms. "We've had nothing but Douglas firs since the day we opened the farm and I think it's time to change that. If you've taught me anything, Kate, it's that change doesn't always have to be scary. Sometimes it just means adding something better to what you already have."

"Like adding me to your payroll," she teased with a wink as she bumped her hip into his in jest.

"Or adding my last name to yours." He returned the spruce to its container and shook off the dirt from his hands. "You know, when we hired you, I thought I was going to be the one doing the teaching. Instead, you've taught me more about life and love than any humble cowboy could ever deserve."

As she looked out over the acreage, heart swelling with gratitude for this farm and for Deacon's family who persevered and prayed to keep this dream alive, Kate fought to hold back her tears. Thankfulness, love, and hope overwhelmed her.

"I love you, Kate," Deacon said, pulling her close under the December night sky. "Merry Christmas."

"Merry Christmas, Deacon." Kate leaned forward and kissed him, knowing she'd found her forever. After years of searching for its purpose, her heart was finally home.

❄

THE END

An Heirloom Christmas

A Lake House Holiday

In the Market for Love

ABOUT THE AUTHOR

Growing up with only a lizard for a pet, Megan Squires now makes up for it by caring for the nearly forty animals on her twelve-acre flower farm in Northern California. A UC Davis graduate, Megan worked in the political non-profit realm prior to becoming a stay-at-home mom. She then spent nearly ten years as an award winning photographer, with her work published in magazines such as Professional Photographer and Click.

In 2012, her creativity took a turn when she wrote and

published her first young adult novel. Megan is both traditionally and self-published and *Christmas at Yuletide Farm* is her twelfth publication. She can't go a day without Jesus, her family and farm animals, and a large McDonald's Diet Coke.

To stay up to date on new releases, sales, and cover reveals, please sign up for Megan's newsletter:

http://subscribe.megansquiresauthor.com

To keep up with Megan online, please visit:

facebook.com/MeganSquiresAuthor

twitter.com/MeganSquires

Made in the USA
Las Vegas, NV
13 December 2020